A Body in the Dust

From the Murder on Mars Series

By Greg Fowlkes

Includes a special preview of
The Blood Red Sands of Mars
Part One from the Murder on Mars Series

A Body in the Dust

© 2020 The Fictional Press
www.TheFictionalPress.com

Published by The Fictional Press

The Fictional Press, an imprint of Intrepid Ink, LLC, provides full publishing services to authors of fiction and non-fiction books, eBooks and websites. From editing to formatting, to publishing, to marketing, Intrepid Ink gets your creative works into the hands of the people who want to read them.

Find out more at www.thefictionalpress.com.

ISBN 13: 978-1-943403-48-6

Printed in the United States of America

CHAPTER 1

Elena was thinking more about home than the road stretching before her. She was some twenty kilometers out from Junction 3, which meant that in less than half an hour she'd be home with Mike and little Miguel, their precocious three year old. Not that she had been gone that long. Her duties on road patrol required her to drive the five hundred kilometers of road between Junction 3 and Junction 2 and back again once a week just as she was required to drive a weekly patrol on the stretch of road between Junction 3 and Junction 4. Given road conditions that limited her average speed to around fifty kilometers an hour, her schedule was to spend Mondays driving to Junction 2, stay there overnight and then drive back on Tuesday. Thursdays she drove to "4", overnighted and drove back on Fridays. The rest of the week she could spend at home unless there was an emergency call.

"Home" was Junction 3, a small settlement originally intended to serve as a way-station on the road. From the original half-dozen inflatable buildings it had expanded into a real community with a population of over a hundred. In addition to the station, which offered travelers meals and a place to sleep, there were now a number of farms and her husband Mike's garage, which in addition to vehicles could repair or build just about anything else. It wasn't what Elena had envisioned for herself when she had left Brownsville, Texas, but she and Mike were making a good life for themselves.

It was getting towards late afternoon and at that season the sun was close to the horizon and almost directly in front of her as she drove west. Not that that posed any great difficulty. The road was well marked and Elena had driven it so many times that she could almost do it in her sleep. Calling it a "road" was perhaps giving it more credit than it deserved. In fact, it was nothing more than a fifty meter wide path that had been graded and had the major obstacles removed. Markers had been placed along the path every hundred meters, enough to keep drivers from getting lost in all but the worst sandstorms. Where the terrain was too rugged, the road went around it, but for the most part it ran straight as an arrow for more than two thousand kilometers in one direction from Mars City and fifteen hundred in the other. There were plans for the road to eventually circle the planet, but lately it seemed those plans had slowed to a crawl.

The road wasn't heavily travelled. Elena considered it a busy day if she passed more than a handful of vehicles on her patrols. Traffic on the road consisted mostly of the scheduled land train that travelled from Mars City to the end of the road and back, and various cargo haulers taking supplies out to the mining camps and returning with the cargos of rare earth ores that were the main reason that Mars had been settled in the first place. Still, the road was the life blood for all the prospectors and settlers in the "Out There."

With the sun in her eyes, Elena was almost on top of it before she spotted the Mars buggy parked to the side of the road fifty or so meters off the center line. It hadn't been there on her way out. A buggy stopped along the side of the road wasn't that unusual. Buggies carried their own self-contained environments, and there were plenty of prospectors that lived for weeks at a time in their buggies.

Still, it would be strange for someone to stop for the night this close to civilization in the form of Junction 3. Most of the prospectors and wildcatters who traveled the Out There were only too eager for company if just for the sound of a human voice other than their own.

Pulling off the road towards the stopped buggy Elena tried to raise it on the radio. There was no response. She couldn't see any signs of life through the front bubble of the buggy, either. With a sigh, she changed channels and placed a call to Junction 3. Fortunately there were relay towers spaced along the road so she wouldn't have to wait for a satellite to be above the horizon.

"Hi, honey. Going to be home soon?" Mike answered. "Miguel is waiting for his mommy, and I've got dinner in the cooker." Mike was a good man, she thought. He seemed unfazed by the burdens of her job.

"Looks like I'm going to be a little late. There's a buggy stopped off the road just past the Kilo 19 marker. I've tried to contact them on radio, but no response."

"You want me to come out there with the wrecker?"

"Not just yet, Mike. I'm going to suit up and check it out. I just wanted to let you know I'd be running late."

"OK, Elena. Let me know if you need anything. I'll expect to hear from you within fifteen minutes."

"Give my love to Miguel."

"I'll do that."

The radio indicated he had hung up. Mike didn't mind her job, but she knew he'd be worrying until she called back. She tried once more to contact the buggy on the radio, but got the same result. She pulled her own buggy to within ten meters of the side of the other opposite the air-lock hatch. She knew most of the prospectors and miners along the road, but she didn't recognize the buggy or the registration numbers stenciled on the side. She surveyed the surrounding area, but with the lengthening shadows she couldn't spot anything out of the ordinary.

She normally didn't wear a surface suit while on patrol. They were uncomfortable and inconvenient to wear for any length of time. Now she had to change into her suit. Slipping out of her coverall, she caught her distorted reflection in the curved windshield of the buggy. Clad in a one piece set of long underwear, she knew she wasn't much to look at. She had barely met the minimum height requirements for the service and had a tendency towards what Mike charitably called "pleasing plumpness." With short black hair and brown skin, she looked what she was, a south Texas Latina.

She took her time suiting up. You didn't rush things like that on Mars. At least the people who were still alive didn't. Mars had a lot of ways to kill people in a hurry. Practice had made the process of donning the suit smooth and efficient, but she didn't take any short cuts. Snapping the helmet into place, she ran through the check-list, verifying that the life-support pack was on-line and functioning. Finally satisfied, she stepped into the small air-lock in the side of the buggy and closed the inner hatch.

The lock cycled and she stepped out onto the surface. It was hard rock swept clean of dust. She had a flashlight in one hand and her service pistol in the other. There were no foot-prints outside the lock, but she noticed her own boots weren't leaving any traces, either.

The hatch was shut, but not secured. On Mars, manners and custom dictated leaving things unlocked in case there was an emergency. She entered the lock and pressed the cycle button. She could hear the flow of air as the lock pressurized. Cautiously she opened the inner hatch. She didn't bother to remove her helmet.

"This is Constable Ortiz. Is anyone to home?" she announced, speaking loudly enough to be heard through her helmet.

There was no answer. The interior lights were off but from the fact that various tell-tales and instruments were lit she could tell that the buggy still had power. She hit the switch for the lights. When they came on she could see that the buggy was empty. Buggies were cramped and there aren't many places to hide. It didn't take much of a search to verify that she was the only one on board.

A quick check of the controls showed that everything on the buggy was working. Just to make sure, she powered the engine up and moved the buggy forward and back a few meters. The buggy hadn't been abandoned due to mechanical problems. She powered the engine down again and sat there in the driver's seat for a moment. That was when she spotted the body. It was laying on the far side of the buggy in the direction opposite from that which she had approached, where it had been hidden by the body of the buggy.

Elena cycled through the airlock again and approached the body. Whoever it was, they were dressed in a surface suit. There were no signs of a struggle, just a few scattered footprints in the red dust. The only anomaly was that the faceplate of the helmet was open. There was no question that the man inside was dead.

CHAPTER 2

Chief Inspector Erik McKernan was running late. That had been too common an occurrence recently. A lot had been going on that required his attention. He was irritable because he wanted to get home. Beth had had the day off and wasn't scheduled back in the hospital's rotation until the following evening. They had planned on a nice dinner at home, and given the always fragile nature of their relationship, it was something that McKernan didn't want to miss. He saved the report he had been working on and was about to stand up when his communicator went off.

"Damn!" He glanced at the ID of the caller and saw that it was Constable Ortiz. One of only two women who worked for him in the UN Trust Authority's Security Service, he'd worked with her on several cases, and he knew she wouldn't be calling without a good reason.

"Elena. McKernan here. What's up?"

"I've got a situation here, sir. I thought you should know about it." The lack of delay in her reply indicated that she was being relayed through the towers along the road rather than through a satellite. McKernan noted the "sir." Though they had worked together closely and were friends, the constable always maintained a certain formality when it concerned business.

"What kind of a situation, constable?" the inspector asked shifting into his official mode.

"I've found a body," Ortiz responded. The constable then went on to explain the circumstances of her discovery.

"Any signs of foul play?"

"Not that I've seen so far, sir. But it's getting dark here now, and I didn't have much time to check things out before the sun set. As far as I can tell, it looks like he just opened his faceplate."

"Suicide?" McKernan queried.

"That's what it looks like, sir," the constable responded.

"Did you know him?"

"I've never seen him before, sir. I don't recognize the buggy, either."

That was surprising, McKernan thought. Ortiz had been stationed out at Junction 3 for almost four years. She was a good cop, smart, yet likable. She knew everyone within five hundred kilometers of Junction 3 and all the residents of that part of Mars knew her. If she didn't recognize the dead man he was either a newcomer or from some other part of Mars.

"Any chance it was an accident? Does it look like he might be a newbie?"

They both knew that the first six months on Mars, before good habits became ingrained, were the most dangerous.

"He doesn't look like he's fresh from Earth, sir. No tan that I could see. His rig looks like it's seen plenty of use. The buggy, too." Of course, that didn't necessarily mean much. Things were *never* discarded on Mars. They were patched and repaired as long as feasible and then they were recycled or repurposed. There were plenty of prospectors wearing suits and driving vehicles that had been on Mars twice as long as their current owners.

"Sounds like you've got a mystery on your hands, constable," McKernan said with a smile. Ortiz liked what she did and had refused reassignment to Mars City because of Mike and Miguel, but that didn't mean that she wouldn't relish the chance to work on something more challenging than patrol duty.

"How do you want me to handle this, sir? Should I wait for you to come out?"

McKernan thought it over. A trip out to Junction 3 would take at least a day if not more and the same time back if he took the land train or a buggy. He might be able to fly out, assuming he could schedule a plane, but that wouldn't be possible until the morning at the earliest. Given his workload, he just couldn't spare the time.

"I've got my hands full at the moment, Elena. Between the upcoming election and a case that I'm working on, I really can't spare a couple of days. You've been around long enough to handle things on your own. I've got every confidence in you. Besides, it sounds like a simple enough case. Death by suicide or stupidity."

"You're probably right, sir," Ortiz replied, though McKernan thought he detected a note of doubt in her voice. It could just be the excitement of having a real case to herself. Still, he trusted the constable's instincts.

"Speaking of the election, are you all prepared?" The election, the first ever on Mars, was to select delegates to a constitutional convention, the first step in the limited home rule that the Trust Authority had finally agreed to. The Security Service had been given the task of handling the voting with the ultimate responsibility for ensuring fair and reliable results falling on McKernan's shoulders. Coordinating a planet wide election with a widely scattered constituency was proving to be no simple matter.

"I've got the blank ballots and the ballot box secured in my office. I know that they are allowing votes to be cast over the commnet, but, at least around Junction 3, most of the people I've talked to are planning on voting in person. I don't know about the rest of the planet, but it sounds like polling day is going to be one big party here."

"Good. It's been a long time coming," McKernan said. The prospect of home rule had been an issue nearly as long as the inspector had been on Mars. "Well, it sounds like you've got things in hand."

"Anything special you want me to do about the body?"

"I suspect that it's too late to do much tonight. Besides, Mike and Miguel are probably waiting for you. Take some images if you haven't already and head on home. See if you can get Mike to help you bring in the body and the buggy in the morning. I'll see that he gets reimbursed at the usual rates. You can send the body in on the next land train for an autopsy."

"Will do, sir."

"Oh, and Elena?"

"Yes, sir?"

"How is little Miguel? Beth would never forgive me if I didn't ask." Beth had been the doctor that had delivered Elena's son. As one of the first children born on Mars, she took a proprietary interest in his welfare.

"He's doing fine, sir. He's walking and talking up a storm. Follows Mike around the shop all day. Give Beth my best."

"I'll do that, Elena. Take care. And let me know if anything interesting turns up."

"I will, sir. Out." The communicator disconnected.

For a moment McKernan wished that he was out with the constable and her mystery, but he had his own concerns, not the least of which was making it home in time for dinner. He logged Ortiz's call and shut down his computer.

Finally finished for the day, McKernan got up and walked out through the station. He paused to exchange a few words with Sergeant Gaeretts, who, as usual, was manning the front desk and would be in command of the overnight shift unless there was a real emergency. Gaeretts was an old Mars hand who had been part of the security force when McKernan had arrived fresh from Earth. The sergeant might not give him all the deference his position dictated, but the Chief Inspector considered him the most valuable member of his small force.

The police station was in the newest part of the city, having moved out of quarters in Hut Town a number of years earlier. The Security Service, typically an afterthought in the Trust Authority's budgeting, had been one of the last U.N. departments to receive quarters in the permanent portion of the city, the part that was built out of fused silica blocks and was buried under a meter of sand in an effort to limit radiation exposure. Before that, the station had been in one of the inflatable huts left over from the first years of the settlement. It had been a wilder time that McKernan looked back on with neither nostalgia nor regret. With a last wave, he walked through the air-tight door of the station to the corridor beyond.

Chapter 3

Constable Ortiz took one last look at the body before covering it with a tarp. Not that she thought that there would be much need for protection. On Mars there were no wild animals to disturb the remains or rains to wash away traces, and with nightfall coming on, the temperatures would quickly drop far lower than any morgue freezer. She weighted the tarp down with rocks in each corner and then headed for home.

By the time Elena reached Junction 3 she was driving by her headlights. Fortunately, it was a well travelled section of the road, and there wasn't much of a chance of her getting lost or wandering off the track.

As she came over the last rise before the settlement, she could spot the lights of the greenhouses that ran for several kilometers on either side away from the road. They gave the place kind of a cheery appearance, at least to someone who'd spent half a dozen years on Mars. During that time, Elena had come to think of Junction 3 as her home, though it was nothing like the Texas where she'd grown up.

The greenhouses were mostly the work of Joseph Huntley, who had the land train concession, though these days he left most of the running of the station to his wife Jenny while he concentrated on farming. He'd started out with one small greenhouse to provide fresh produce for the small dining room that served passengers on the train. The operation had proved such a success that it had grown continuously over the years and supplied several of the mining operations in the area as well as Station Alpha, the scientific research center to the north of the junction. The land train even took some of his produce into Mars City. He had added hogs and chickens to the mix and learned to make his own bacon and sausage. Huntley employed a couple of dozen people on the farm, and his success had led to several other farms springing up around Junction 3. The presence of so many people had caused several other businesses to locate there, and little by little, Junction 3 was taking on the aspects of a village.

It had changed a lot since she had first been stationed there to patrol the surrounding country. The buildings that flanked either side of the road were made of fused glass blocks now rather than the pneumatic huts that had formerly occupied that space. They extended for a couple of hundred meters along the road, too. The land train station had been expanded into a real hotel and miners would start showing up Friday night for a weekend of rest and recreation, though things never got as rowdy as they did at the far end of Hut Town in Mars City.

Elena parked her buggy across the road from the station in front of the big building where her husband worked. She looked with pride at the sign on front that simply said "MIKE'S." They were making a good life for themselves, she thought, better than she had expected when she was growing up in Brownsville.

She hadn't bothered to change out of her surface suit, so all she had to do was put on her helmet before entering the buggy's airlock. But even though she only had a few meters to cross, she went through the checklist to make sure of suit integrity.

The airlock into the shop was bigger than the one on the buggy, which only meant that it took longer to cycle. Elena waited impatiently until the light turned green and she could get inside. She had barely gotten the door shut behind her when she felt an impact and looked down to see her three year old son wrap his arms around the leg of her surface suit.

"Mommy, Mommy!"

She picked him up, glad for the lower gravity of Mars. Her son was growing up fast. Only the fact that she still had her helmet on kept her from kissing him.

She had just put him down so she could take off the helmet when Mike appeared. He'd been underneath a big excavator that he'd pulled into the pressurized service bay so he didn't have to wear a suit while working on it. She noticed a smudge of grease on his forehead as he embraced her. His kiss was awkward because of the neck ring of her suit.

"Glad to see you. I'll have dinner on the table by the time you've changed."

Mike didn't usually say much, but then he didn't have to.

"You should wash up yourself," she admonished. "And Miguel, as well." Miguel had taken to following his father around the shop while he worked. He'd picked up his father's tendency to attract dirt, too.

Mike grinned and picked up the boy, slinging him over his shoulder.

She went into the alcove off of the service bay where they kept the suit lockers. She got out of the suit, stowed it in her locker along with her helmet, and changed into the jump suit that she kept there. She knew that it didn't do anything to improve her figure, but then nothing much would. She hooked the suit's life support pack to the charging station so that it would have full batteries and air tanks in the morning.

Mike had built their living quarters onto the shop, a living area with a galley kitchen, a bathroom and two small bedrooms, one for Miguel, and one for Mike and her. It wasn't large, but it felt cozy. They'd hung pictures on the wall of wild places on Earth for Miguel, though chances were he'd never set foot on the planet. Elena sometimes wondered whether it would have been better if they had put up pictures of Mars, instead.

Mike was dishing up dinner as she walked in. Since they'd been together he'd become a decent cook, though he never made things spicy enough for her taste. Still, it was nice having someone who took care of her, even if only in small ways. She liked to cook, herself, but being away four days out of the week limited her chances. It was too bad, really, because she could get fresh vegetables grown right across the road.

"So what did you do today, Miguel?" she asked as she sat down.

"I helped daddy with a ex-cavator," the boy said proudly. "It needs a new hydraulic clutch." He might not be four yet, but he'd already picked up a lot hanging around with his dad. Elena was happy to see it. Her own father hadn't been around much when she was growing up.

"I'm sure you did, Miguel. I can tell from the grease under your fingernails," Elena said.

Miguel looked sheepishly at his fingers.

"Daddy said you found a body," he blurted out to change the subject.

"Yes, I did. That's why I was late."

"How did he die?" Miguel asked with a child's curiosity.

"He had some sort of suit malfunction," she answered. She had never tried to shield the boy from the realities of living on Mars. Soon enough, he'd have to be responsible for his own safety, and she wanted him to be ready for it.

"What sort of function?"

"His face plate was open when I found him," she responded.

"Eww. That's bad."

"Yes it is.

"Any sign of what happened?" Mike asked with concern.

"No. It looked like he was by himself when it happened."

They both knew what that meant.

"Who was it?"

"I don't know. I didn't recognize him, and I don't remember seeing the buggy before. McKernan wanted to know if you could go out to the site tomorrow to bring in the buggy and the body. It's only about twenty kilometers down the road, so it shouldn't take that long. You'll get paid."

"Sure. It shouldn't be a problem."

"Jenny can watch Miguel while we're gone," Elena said.

"Will I need to take the wrecker?" Mike asked. "If so I should fuel it up tonight."

"No. I checked out the buggy while I was there. It seemed to be working just fine."

"Kind of a strange place to—" he looked at Miguel "—you know."

Miguel looked from his father to his mother. He knew when they were trying to hide something from him.

"Yeah. A lot of things about it seem strange," Elena said thoughtfully.

"Like what?" Mike asked.

"Oh, like, who was he? What was he doing there? Where did he come from? It wasn't a company buggy, or at least it didn't have a company logo on it. And I thought I knew all the prospectors and wildcatters around here. You haven't heard of anyone new working in the Out There, have you?"

"Nope. None of my customers has said anything about anyone new, and you know how most of them love to gossip."

"Yeah, that's why I think it strange. He had to have come from somewhere."

"Why?" Miguel interrupted with the curiosity of a three year old.

"Because he did," Elena replied. "Now isn't it time for you to get ready for bed?"

"Aw."

"Scoot, young man. I'll be there in a moment to read you a story."

"OK."

After the boy had left Mike asked, "So you think this guy just decided to open his faceplate?"

"Do you mean do I think he committed suicide? I just don't know. Maybe we'll find out tomorrow," Elena said uncertainly.

"Why don't you go in to Miguel," Mike said. "I can clean up the dishes."

"I knew there was a reason I picked you," Elena commented, kissing her husband on the forehead before going into Miguel's bedroom.

CHAPTER 4

McKernan's path home took him down a corridor leading towards the center of the city. The walls of the corridor were made of the same fused silica blocks that were used for almost all construction on Mars. The glossy, almost colorless walls of the hall were broken at intervals by airlocks leading to the various administrative offices of the Trust Authority. Nearly a quarter of the ten thousand or so inhabitants of the city were employed in some fashion by the Trust Authority. Not for the first time, McKernan wondered how that would change when home rule was finally granted.

After a hundred meters, the corridor opened out into an open space ten meters high, thirty meters wide, and over a hundred meters long. There was an air-tight door marking the transition, but this far inside the city it normally stood open. On the official plans of the city the space was labeled "The Grand Concourse." Mostly people just called it the Concourse. Normally, it had all the charm of a third rate shopping mall back on Earth, a large, mostly empty space, colorless like the corridors that fed into it, with a few potted bushes scattered around to lend a semblance of life. However, since the U.N. had agreed, at least in principle, to granting some measure of local control to Mars, the Concourse had become a center for a civic life that had been previously largely absent. The walls were plastered with the campaign posters of the various candidates for the constitutional assembly and kiosks for the two major political parties had appeared.

The Inspector had been amazed at how rapidly people had fallen into the two camps, the Pragmatists or red party and the Futurists or the greens. Considering that there wasn't actually a great deal of difference in the platforms and positions of the two groups, it was hard to see why people were becoming so passionate with their loyalties, but passionate they were. Fortunately, the relations between the two parties had so far remained largely civil.

The Concourse had become the focal point of discussions and debates on the topic, and at this hour of the early evening little knots of people were gathered in conversation. McKernan, given his position as the person responsible for overseeing the election, had tried to remain publicly neutral on the subject, even though privately he was firmly in the Pragmatists' camp. As he passed through the Concourse he made a point of being impartial in his greetings. He knew how important it was to maintain the people's trust. The responses to his greetings were uniformly polite and cordial; as a long time resident, the chief inspector was both well known and respected.

He was almost relieved when he entered the corridor on the far side of the Concourse that led to Hut Town's Corridor B. This corridor, though little different in appearance than the one that housed the administrative offices, was populated by the private businesses and shops that provided goods and services to the mining corporations and their employees. It was the mining corporations that had provided the real reason for the settlement of Mars, and it was the rare earths that they shipped to Earth that paid for all the things that couldn't be produced or grown on Mars.

At the end of the corridor he entered an airlock. This was the real point of division between what people were starting to think of as Mars City and what they had always referred to as Hut Town. It always struck McKernan as curious that people had started to capitalize Hut Town before they had done so with Mars City. Officially, at least to the Trust Authority, neither name existed. Hut Town was the "Original Settlement" and Mars City was the "Permanent Settlement," but people rarely pay attention to official policy in matters of language.

Hut Town had long been used to refer to the far end of the corridors where the bars, flop houses and bordellos that catered to miners and prospectors in town for a spree were concentrated. Gradually, the name had been extended to all of the huts that had been used in the early days of Mars, huts made from an inflatable skin stiffened with a thin layer of sprayed on foam and connected by long tubes constructed in the same manner. When the Trust Authority had started to build more permanent quarters out of silica blocks, Mars City proper, the corporate and government departments had abandoned those huts. But nothing on Mars was ever discarded or left unused. At first, it had been the saloons and bawdy houses that had filled the vacuum, but soon it was anyone looking for a cheap space to occupy or just more living room. Hut Town was where those who weren't employed by the Trust Authority or one of the corporations mostly lived and where small time private enterprises flourished.

McKernan had quickly grown tired of the small cubicle he had been assigned in the Trust Authority's male dormitory, and within a year of arriving on Mars he had taken over a hut from a prospector who had struck it rich and headed back to Earth. That transaction, like all of the property transfers in Hut Town, hadn't been official.

Technically, the Trust Authority maintained title to everything in Hut Town, one of the main points of contention driving the demand for home rule. McKernan, like most of his neighbors, had put a great deal of time and money into his hut, and, like them, he wanted a clear title to what he considered his home.

The corridor that he walked down was quite different than the one he had just left. This one was cylindrical, the curve of the walls quite apparent. Exposed wiring and plumbing ran down the sides, and the floor was a metal grating under which was a space used for more plumbing and cabling. The floor in the first section sloped upward slightly; most of the corridor was on the surface, not buried. Airlocks pierced the wall at intervals. In this section, close to Mars City, there were mostly businesses behind the hatches. The airlocks were always kept closed, as the walls of the corridor were thin and vulnerable. The corridor was also cold. The insulation was thin, and no one was willing to pay for heat in space that wasn't occupied.

Yet despite all the roughness, despite the cold, dry air, despite the ever present dust that lay everywhere, the corridors of Hut Town lacked the sterility of Mars City. To one familiar with what lay behind the airlocks, as McKernan was, there was a vibrant culture evolving here, a peculiarly Martian culture.

McKernan passed through an airlock at the end of the section of corridor and into another length of corridor. Corridor B, one of the five main corridors that made up Hut Town, was mostly occupied by residences once one got out of the sections nearest Mars City. The section where McKernan lived was one of the more respectable ones. Extra insulation had been sprayed on, the lighting was all kept in working order, and there was even a neighborhood association that handled maintenance and order.

He reached the airlock of his hut and cycled through. Inside, things were different. It was warmer, the air more humid. There were the aromas of cooking and the scents of the vegetables and herbs that grew at the far end of the hut. The furniture was makeshift but comfortable, and artwork occupied the walls and shelves, artwork that owed nothing to Earth.

"Sorry I'm late," McKernan said as he took off his sidearm and set it on the table that stood just inside the airlock.

"That's okay," Beth said. "Dinner won't be ready for a few minutes. Trouble at work?"

"No. It's just that Ortiz called as I was leaving. She's found a body along the road."

"A body?" Beth asked more out of curiosity than alarm.

"Looks like a suicide. He just opened his faceplate."

Beth, being a doctor, had had firsthand experience with the many ways Mars had of killing a man and grown used to the dangers of living on Mars. Her mind quickly turned to other matters. "How is Elena? And Miguel?"

"They're both fine." Beth treated Miguel, the first baby she had delivered on Mars, as an unofficial nephew.

"Good. I'm glad to hear that. Miguel will be due for a physical soon. Why don't you mix us a couple of drinks before dinner?"

CHAPTER 5

On the trip out the next morning to recover the body, Elena let her husband Mike drive the buggy. Driving was, after all, a husband's prerogative, even if she did spend nearly half her days driving back and forth on this same stretch of road. Not that Mike wasn't a competent driver. On the contrary, he could, and had, operated just about every type of vehicle one could find on Mars and could probably repair almost any of them provided he had the parts or the materials to make them.

Actually, Elena was enjoying her time in the passenger seat. Since little Miguel had been born they hadn't had that much time alone together, not that she minded, but it was nice just to be able to relax for a little bit watching Mike as his strong hands operated the controls of the buggy. He was a quiet, shy man, slim but with the wiry build of so many long time Martians. It had been a surprise when he had first approached her at a small party at Junction 3 some five years earlier. Even on Mars where men outnumbered women seven to one, she knew she wasn't much to look at, short and squat, with a brown face and coarse black hair cut short because it was easier to deal with under the helmet of a surface suit. But he had asked her to dance, which they both did badly. And here she was on her second three year contract on Mars, knowing that she would never be going back to Earth again.

By Martian standards, Mike could be considered quite a catch. On a planet where what you could do was much more important than who you were, a man who could fix all the equipment that was necessary for survival in the alien environment was someone to be respected and cultivated. Mike had used his position as mechanic at Junction 3 to build a nice repair business that drew customers from a thousand kilometers around. It hadn't made him exactly rich, but he had his own shop and had been able to build them a nice cozy home to live in. So what if it was built of fused silica bricks and buried under a meter of sand. It was theirs, which was more than she'd ever had growing up back in Texas.

A passing road marker snapped Elena out of her reverie.

"That's the Kilometer 19 marker. It should be just a little bit ahead on the left," she informed Mike, sitting up a little straighter in the buggy's seat.

Mike slowed the buggy, not that there'd be much chance of him missing it. The terrain was flat and open along this stretch of the road, and there wasn't much between the road and the horizon.

Mike drove on for another couple of minutes. They should have spotted the buggy by now. He could tell that Elena was getting uneasy. When they passed the Kilo 20 marker he turned and asked, "Are you sure that it was between 19 and 20?" Even as he asked, he knew it was a stupid question, but where was the buggy they'd been searching for?

"I know where I saw it, Mike. Turn around." She had used her policeman's voice, not that of a wife. Mike slowed the buggy further, took a wide turn and headed back the way they came. Elena was staring intently, not at the width of the road, but at the hills in the background. They repassed the Kilo 20 marker and had gone about 700 meters farther when she ordered him to stop.

He pulled the buggy about 20 meters off the side of the road and came to a stop, the front of the buggy pointing out away from the road. Outside of their buggy there wasn't anything man-made in sight.

"This is where I found him," Elena insisted.

"Are you sure?" Mike asked. "It was late and one chunk of road looks a lot like another along here."

"I know where I was, Mike." He recognized the stubborn certainty in the tone of her voice, and he knew his wife well enough to know that until there was proof to the contrary he should believe her.

"Are you sure he was dead?"

"His faceplate was open," Elena replied tersely. Given the air pressure and temperature on Mars, that was enough explanation.

"What do you think happened then? Do you think someone drove off with the buggy during the night?" Theft wasn't common in the Out There, the part of Mars away from the few settlements. People's lives were too dependent on their supplies and equipment to tolerate it. But it was possible that someone investigating a buggy parked by the side of the road might consider it legitimate salvage if they had found the body of its owner lying in the dust not far away. They might even be planning to turn it in to the authorities, but if so, why hadn't they driven it to Junction 3 which was certainly the closest outpost of civilization. No one had arrived during the night and they hadn't passed anyone on the way out.

"I don't know, Mike, but I don't like it. I'm getting out and look around."

Elena got up out of her seat and began to put on her surface suit. Mike started to join her, but the space in the buggy was cramped, and he had to wait for her to finish.

"I'm coming, too," he said. She hesitated a moment and then nodded. From long habit, they checked each other's helmet seals and life support packs without even thinking about it. Mike noted that Elena had strapped her service pistol to the outside of her suit. He was more alarmed when she unclipped a riot gun from where it was clamped next to the airlock.

The airlocks on Mars buggies were only large enough to accommodate one person at a time. Mike didn't argue about who was going to go first. This was Elena's job, and he had only come along to drive the other buggy back. He waited for the lock to cycle her through and then stepped into the narrow confines to make his own exit.

When it had cycled, he opened the outer hatch and stepped onto the surface. Elena was waiting for him, gazing out into the distance. The shotgun was held loosely in her right hand ready to be swung up if needed.

Looking around, there wasn't much to see. Mike looked down at the ground. It was hard-packed stone with only a light coating of wind-blown dust on the surface. It would be hard to spot tracks with that kind of surface.

"What now?"

"We look for tracks," Elena answered curtly. "I'll go this way, you go that."

"How far?"

"No more than fifty meters. I'm pretty sure that this is the place I found it."

"What about the body? Shouldn't we be able to spot it?"

"We should. I covered it with a tarp. One of the emergency ones." The tarps were colored a bright blue with a fluorescent green boarder, two colors chosen to stand out against the reddish terrain of Mars.

They started walking out in opposite directions, their eyes on the ground in front of them. They were outside of the area that had been swept clean for the road, but it was still fairly flat, the surface broken only by the occasional loose rock. They had almost walked out to the fifty meter limit when Mike heard Elena over his radio, "Mike. Over here."

He walked to join her. Running can be precarious in the lighter gravity of Mars, particularly in a surface suit. When he got up to where she stood, he looked down. There was a small depression in which some dust had gathered, maybe a few centimeters worth. Right across the center of the depression was the track of a buggy wheel. It was always hard to tell the age of tracks on Mars because, with the low air pressure, dust didn't blow around much, but it looked fresh. Of course, that could mean it was a day old or three months.

There was no way to tell which buggy had made the track, they all used the same basic wheel and tread design. It could have been the dead man's buggy or Elena's. Or someone else's. What was clear, though, is that someone had driven off the road here, and recently.

"This the spot then?" Mike asked.

"Yeah," Elena confirmed. "The buggy must have been parked just about over there." She was pointing to a spot about twenty meters from where they stood. "The body was just a little beyond."

They walked towards the spot, keeping a close eye on the ground, but neither of them spotted further traces. Elena stopped and stared at a spot in the dust. As far as Mike could see, there was nothing to distinguish it from any other spot.

"When I covered him with a tarp, I used four rocks to weight the corners. Those rocks." Mike looked down. There were four rocks, about a kilo each, spaced to make a square about two meters on a side, the size of the tarp.

"OK. This is where the body lay. The buggy was just over there. You know it, and I believe you. But there doesn't seem to be much in the way of evidence, Elena. What do we do next?"

"We search. Look for clues. Anything. How should I know? I'm nothing more than a glorified interplanetary traffic cop." Mike knew that Elena was kicking herself over all the things she could have done differently, like bringing the body in last night or asking someone to come out and join her. Which was all great in hindsight, but who would have expected someone to walk off with a body?

"Don't beat yourself up, Elena. You had no reason to expect any problems. McKernan himself told you it could wait until morning."

"I know that, Mike, but it's my crime scene that's been messed up."

Mike just smiled and started looking around. Elena stood there for a moment, and then joined him.

It was Mike who found it. There was a little ravine about five meters from where the body had lain. It wasn't much, less than a meter deep, maybe a trace of a little stream back from the time when Mars had liquid water, perhaps just an unevenness in the ground. At the bottom of the ravine some of the dust and rocks had been pushed into a little mound. It was hardly noticeable, except for the traces where the soil had been scraped up.

Mike scuffed at it with his toe. With the sand scraped away he could see bright blue. He scuffed some more. Elena came over to see what had caught his attention.

"The tarp," Mike said unnecessarily. He sounded like a dog that had just uncovered a bone.

"Yes, dear," the constable said. "It's a tarp. My tarp." She reached down and pulling on a corner freed it from the soil that had been used to cover it.

"What I don't understand is why they didn't take it with them? Or just leave it lay?" Mike asked.

"Because of this, Mike," she said as she shook out the tarp. Stenciled neatly across the edge were the words "Property of Elena Ortiz," words that Mike had placed there himself. "They didn't want to risk getting caught with it, but they didn't want to leave any evidence behind, either."

"So what do we do now?"

"What *I* do now is call the Chief Inspector," Elena said ruefully.

CHAPTER 6

McKernan was standing in the bullpen of the police station looking over the incident reports from the previous night when the call came in. Gaeretts was leaning against the counter of the front desk drinking a cup of what passed for coffee on Mars. A quick glance at the ID on his comm told the inspector that it was Ortiz.

"It's Elena," he told Gaeretts before hitting "accept."

"Morning, Constable. Have you identified your body yet?"

"That's just it, sir. I don't have a body."

McKernan gave a quick glance at the clock on the wall. Ortiz had always been one of his most diligent constables. "I would have thought that you'd be out there already."

"Oh, I'm out at the site where I found the body, sir. It's just that the body is missing and so is the buggy."

"Any chance that the guy wasn't dead?" McKernan asked.

"Not unless he could breathe vacuum, sir. I saw the open faceplate."

McKernan didn't bother to apologize for his question. "Any chance someone else found the body and picked it up?"

"It's possible, sir, but it was late when I left the scene. Not many people travel the road at night. Besides, if they had found the body, why didn't they just bring it in to

Junction 3? Everyone knows I'm there, and it's less than twenty kilometers away."

"That does seem odd," McKernan agreed.

"There's one other thing. Last night I covered the body with a tarp and placed some rocks on it to hold it down. This morning the rocks were still there where I put them, but the tarp was missing. Mike found it in a ravine nearby buried under some sand. It had been intentionally hidden."

"Foul play?"

"The tarp had my name stenciled on it. Whoever took the body and drove off in the buggy didn't want to be seen with it. I can't think of any logical reason for someone honest to do that."

"What about the registration number? Did you get that last night?" All vehicles on Mars were required to have a number painted on the side where they'd be clearly visible from a distance.

"Of course," Ortiz answered a little testily. "I took a picture of it before I got out of my buggy. I just ran it through the computer. It was bogus. The number was valid, alright, but it belongs to an excavator that was junked a couple of years ago."

With a real number stenciled on the side the buggy wouldn't have attracted attention, but it would be impossible to track the owners using it.

"Sounds like you've got a real mystery on your hands, Constable," McKernan said sympathetically.

"What do you want me to do, sir?" Ortiz asked.

"I'm afraid that you're on your own for the moment, Elena. At least until you can turn up some more evidence. I can't really spare anyone to help out right now. I *can* have Kaminsky cover your next road patrol if you want. He'll be working the road from Junction 5 to Junction 4, anyway. I'd rather have you clear up this business than driving back and forth."

"Yes, sir. Thank you."

"Good. If you need any logistical support, work with Gaeretts. And let me know as soon as you find something."

"I'll do that, sir."

"Good-bye." McKernan hung up.

Gaeretts gave him a raised eyebrow. "What's up?"

"That body and buggy Elena found by the side of the road last night has gone missing. It was late, so she was going to bring it in this morning. Someone seems to have beaten her to it. When she and Mike drove out the body was gone and so was the buggy."

"That's pretty weird," Gaeretts remarked laconically.

"To put it mildly. It looks like whoever did it also tried to cover their tracks. They hid the tarp Elena had covered the body with. Someone is up to no good, we just don't know who or why. I want you to give Ortiz any help you can."

"Sure thing, boss," Gaeretts agreed.

"Anything in here I need to know about?" McKernan asked holding the tablet with the overnight incident report.

"Well, we had another one last night." The way he said it made it clear what he was referring to.

"Another one? Where?"

"Out at the end of Corridor C," Gaeretts answered. The end of Corridor C was where the bars and bordellos were concentrated. "A welder name of Dan Petersen in from one of the camps. One minute he's drinking with a couple of buddies and the next he's trying to exit an airlock without a surface suit. Fortunately, his buddies weren't as drunk as he was and were able to stop him before the lock cycled. After it was over they called it in and I sent Ferris to handle it. It was all he could do to subdue him. He had to have the two buddies help him get him to the hospital. He's there now."

"Sure it's the same thing?" Mckernan asked. "He wasn't just drunk?"

"Not according to the statements that his friends made to Ferris. Petersen had all the signs. One minute he's behaving normally, then the next he's acting like he has no idea that he's on Mars and is doing his best to get himself killed."

"Did his friends mention any signs of instability?"

"Nope. They seemed pretty shook up about the whole thing. All they told Ferris was that Petersen was two years into his contract. He was good at his job and got along with everyone he worked with. One of them did mention that he'd been kind of homesick the last few weeks, but they just chalked that up to his coming up on his two year anniversary on Mars." Gaeretts commented, "That seems to happen to most first timers."

McKernan just nodded. Over the last three months there had been nearly a dozen similar cases, four of which hadn't been as lucky as Petersen and ended up dead. For lack of a better explanation, it was presumed to be some new drug that was turning normally cautious people into delusional psychotics who acted as if they were unaware of their surroundings, something that could easily get you killed on Mars. It was becoming a major problem for McKernan and his department, and with his attention focused on the upcoming elections, it couldn't be happening at a worse time.

"Is he still at the hospital?"

"Yeah. Ferris told the doc to hold him until he got the word from you. Not that it sounds like the guy is in any shape to be let wandering around."

"I'll go over there later. Anything else happen last night?"

"The usual. A couple of miners ended up in the drunk tank. Two prospectors went at it with knives over a working girl at Bertha's. Neither one was seriously hurt, though the woman got a black eye out of it. And we've had our first case of political violence."

"Oh?" McKernan said, raising an eyebrow.

"Yeah. A couple of people who should have known better got to arguing about whether there should be a clause supporting terraforming in the new constitution. The Pragmatist, who's a chemist with Anglo-Martian, said the idea was premature and "a needless distraction," and the Futurist, who is a machinist with Interplanetary, said it was vital if we were ever to have 'a better Mars.' They got into a shouting match on the Concourse. That ended up with one shoving the other and then they ripped up each other's posters. The two of them gathered quite a crowd until Ferris broke it up."

"Anyone hurt?"

"No," the sergeant said with a laugh. "They were mostly just blowing off steam. Ferris made them shake hands and sent them home."

"That's all we need. We haven't even elected the delegates to the convention yet and already we have people fighting about something that won't happen in their lifetimes even if it *is* technically possible and we *could* come up with the funds to pay for it. It's not like we don't have enough real problems to worry about," McKernan vented.

"Careful, Inspector. You're starting to sound like a Pragmatist. What will the Greens say if they hear you talk like that?"

"Politics!"

"It's the coming thing," Gaeretts commented.

"Lord help us," McKernan said shaking his head. "If you need me, I'll be over at the hospital checking up on our apolitical loony."

CHAPTER 7

After McKernan had hung up, Elena stood in silence for a moment staring at the ground.

"What now?" came Mike's voice over her helmet's speaker.

"I take some images, do a search for evidence, and then I guess we drive home. Sorry I got you out on a wild goose chase," Elena said apologetically.

"It's OK, Elena," Mike said cheerfully. "I've enjoyed taking the morning off. I don't get much down time."

They spent the next half hour walking the scene and taking images of anything that might be useful, which wasn't much. There were some tire tracks that might have been those of any buggy. There was the ravine where the tarp had been buried, the four rocks that she had used to weight it down, and that was about it. The hard ground where she had found the body hadn't revealed an impression. Elena placed the tarp in a plastic evidence bag, though she doubted that it would yield anything in the way of evidence. It was unlikely that whoever had taken the body had handled it with their bare hands. Not that Mars had much in the way of a crime lab, anyway. They might be able to take fingerprints, but that was close to the limits of what could be done on Mars. DNA samples had to be sent back to Earth for analysis, a process that was expensive and time consuming and rarely used.

When they got back in the buggy, Mike took the controls. Without asking, he knew that his wife needed some time to think.

As they drove back to Junction 3, Elena stared out the front window. After they had gone a few kilometers Mike asked, "What's bothering you, Elena?"

"I'm just kicking myself. My first chance to work a major case alone and I go and lose the body."

"That wasn't your fault. McKernan, himself, told you to leave it until morning. You couldn't have done much last night, anyway."

"I could have parked the buggy and spent the night."

"And miss time with Miguel?"

Elena smiled at her husband. He knew her weak spots and how to cheer her up.

"You're right, Mike."

"You're still bothered, though, aren't you?"

"Yeah. I can't even prove that there ever was a body."

"You've got the image of the buggy that you took. That's proof."

"Yeah, an image of a retired registration number on the side of what could be any buggy. It's not even a very good image. It doesn't show the whole buggy. I parked my buggy too close. And the body was lying on the far side, so I don't have an image of that. And the fact that the image was time stamped doesn't mean much. You know how easy it can be to spoof something like that."

"McKernan won't think you're faking evidence. He knows you too well for that."

"Sure, the inspector believes me, but that won't mean much if we try to hold someone responsible. Without a body there's really nothing to show there's anything worth investigating. The department just doesn't have enough resources to go chasing phantoms."

"So? Find the body. How hard can it be? This is Mars. It's not like whoever took it is going to be able to take it off planet. It's not that easy to get rid of a buggy, either. What can be hidden can be found."

"It's not that simple, Mike. This isn't some treasure hunt where 'X' marks the spot."

"Isn't it? Maybe you don't have a treasure map to guide you, but you know this part of Mars as well as anyone. Besides, I've got faith in you."

She looked over to where Mike sat in the driver's seat. He wasn't exactly handsome by Earth standards. His face was too sharp, his forehead a bit too high, the brownish hair on top was already starting to thin and turn grey. He was shy with strangers and quiet with friends, but when he said something, he meant it, and if he said he had faith in her, he did.

She smiled and said, "OK, I'll find the damn body."

"See."

They drove the rest of the way back to Junction 3 in silence, but Elena was busy thinking rather than blaming herself.

Back at her desk in the little cubicle at Junction 3 that served as her office Elena tried to figure out what her next step would be. The registration number, J-973, was a dead end. Or was it? It had originally belonged on an excavator at one of the mining camps. The excavator had gotten caught in a landslide several years back and hadn't been worth repairing. What could be salvaged for parts, and on Mars that would have meant just about everything, had probably been taken off it long ago. She doubted that there was even a stripped chassis left to oxidize in the thin Martian atmosphere. That didn't really matter, though, because the excavator hadn't been anything like a Mars buggy, and the only connection to the body was the number.

But why pick that number to paint on the side of the buggy she had found? The answer was because it was a perfectly good number. Someone seeing it would have no reason to think that it wasn't the legitimate registration, and by picking a number that had been retired, whoever had painted it on the buggy wouldn't have to worry about some embarrassing coincidence like two buggy's with identical numbers being in the same place, or someone recognizing the number as belonging to someone else. And that meant two things. First, the person who had put it on the side of the buggy would have had to have known that the number had been retired. But second, and more importantly, the only reason to fake a registration number was because whoever did it was involved in something illegal, or at least questionable. Why else use a fake number? There wasn't any fee for getting a number; they were issued on demand in a sequence as a matter of course.

There had to be some sort of connection between the defunct excavator and the body. If she could only figure out how the owner of the buggy had known that the number wasn't in use, she might be able to figure out who "they" had been.

It occurred to Elena that maybe the connecting link was that the dead man had been around at the time that the excavator had been put out of action. A quick check of the excavator's registration record showed that it had been assigned to Northern & Big Sky Mining, a Canadian company with several large mining operations on Mars. It was certainly possible that the dead man had worked for the company at the time of the excavator accident. It was even possible that he was still an employee. She sent a quick text message to Northern's operations office inquiring if any of their workers had gone missing. It might take some time to get a reply, but it was worth making the effort.

With the awareness of this possible connection, she felt encouraged. Maybe the case wasn't as hopeless as it had appeared. But were there other angles could she get on it?

She got on her comm and placed a call to Gaeretts.

"Elena. I understand you managed to lose a body," the sergeant answered sarcastically. For some reason, the usually gruff Gaerretts always treated her like a favorite niece.

"I didn't lose it, it was stolen. That's why I'm calling."

"What can I do for you? The chief said to give you any help I could."

"I need to get any satellite images of that section of road and the surrounding area. Say between Junction 3 and the 50 kilometer marker. Particularly during the hour or two before and after sundown."

There were a number of artificial satellites orbiting Mars for a variety of purposes such as communications, surveying, and keeping track of the weather, what there was of it. With luck, one of them might have captured something helpful.

"I'll see what I can do. Don't hold your breath, though. Coverage is pretty hit or miss unless you put in an order ahead of time."

"Well, anything you can dig up would be a help."

"OK. It may will take awhile. I'll send it along as soon as I can. Anything else?"

"You might put out the word asking if anyone has seen a buggy with registration number J-973 lately."

"Will do, though I thought the chief said that the number was bogus."

"It is, but there was a buggy driving around with it plastered on the side. I'd love to know where it had been."

"OK. I'll pass the word along to the rest of the constables. The road train crews, too."

"Thanks," Elena said. As she hung up she noted the time. It was nearly lunch. She had agreed to meet Mike in the diner, but there was one thing she had to do before that.

She wasn't much of a graphic designer, but she managed to work up a poster that she hoped would catch people's eye:

J-973
Anyone with information
On a vehicle with this registration
Please contact Constable Ortiz

She printed off a half dozen copies that she could post in the diner and the other public parts of Junction 3. It was a low tech approach, but sooner or later most of the people who lived within a few hundred kilometers of Junction 3 would see it, and she might get lucky.

CHAPTER 8

As McKernan walked the short distance down the corridor to the hospital he considered the problem of the psychotic episodes. In theory, at least, everyone who came to Mars had to undergo full medical screening, including psychological testing. One would expect them to be the healthiest human population ever, mostly young, fit, and well adjusted. Of course, in practice, it didn't always work out that way. The strain of living under the harsh conditions on Mars, the confined quarters, the hostile environment on the surface, the fact that a man couldn't survive for more than a few seconds outside without a surface suit, adversely affected some people; caused them to break down. Surprisingly, it didn't happen that often, but it did happen. Usually when it did happen, it was detected, either by the individual or by their coworkers, and if the problem was severe enough the person was shipped home. In the few cases where it wasn't detected in time, well, Mars had dozens of ways to kill you.

But this latest epidemic, and McKernan was beginning to think of it in those terms, seemed to strike without warning. People who had appeared normal would suddenly act as if they had no idea of where they were; would act as if they were somewhere back on Earth. The consequences of that could too easily prove fatal, and in several cases they already had.

For a moment he wondered if Ortiz's missing body was another case. That might explain the open faceplate. The man might have opened it thinking that there was a breathable atmosphere outside. Of course, without a body, there was no way to tell what had happened, or even if anything had happened at all. Not that he had any doubts about Constable Ortiz or her truthfulness.

Of course, the whole business had to blow up at a time when he had the least resources to devote to the problem. His department was small, a few dozen constables to police a planet with a surface area as great as the land area of Earth. Even in the best of times his department was stretched thin, but with the election for delegates to the constitutional convention fast approaching they were particularly hard pressed. Not only were there the little flare ups of political zeal like the shoving match on the concourse the previous night, but his department was the one that was going to be held responsible if anything went wrong with the distribution, collection, and counting of the ballots. He was only too well aware that everyone from the Trust Authority on down was watching his actions, waiting for some misstep on his part if the results should end up not to their liking.

The inspector was almost relieved when he arrived at the hospital. At least the psychosis epidemic was something concrete to deal with.

Since the beginning of his relationship with Beth, he had become well known to the hospital staff. They were no longer surprised by his visits which weren't always of a professional nature. The nurse at the reception station smiled as he came in.

"Dr. Haestert is busy with a patient right now, Inspector."

"Actually, it's Dr. Greenwood that I want to see. Is he in?"

The nurse raised an eyebrow. "He's probably back in the lab. Go on through." She pressed the button to open the door to the inner workings of the hospital.

McKernan knew his way around well enough to find the lab area. Greenwood was standing at a computer terminal, focused on the display. He didn't seem surprised when he looked up at the sound of the inspector's approach.

"I've been expecting you to poke your head in, Inspector."

Greenwood was head of the hospital staff and senior medical officer on Mars. He'd been on planet nearly as long as McKernan, and accepted the fact that he'd never return to Earth. He could be abrasive at times, curt when busy, but he was efficient and extremely competent at what he did.

"How's your patient?" They both knew which patient McKernan was referring to.

"I've got him sedated for the moment. I don't think he poses any immediate danger to himself or others."

"Is he the same as the others?"

"If you mean, is he delusional? The answer is yes. I was able to talk to him when they brought him in last night. As far as he was concerned he was back on Earth. Aruba, in fact. He was very specific about that. He was convinced that if he just went through the airlock at the end of Corridor C he'd step out onto the beach there. Nothing I could say would convince him otherwise. He had no idea that he was on Mars, and even when I told him where he was he refused to believe me."

"His trip to the 'beach' would have been fatal." McKernan commented.

"Fortunately, he was with a couple of friends who stopped him. Considering their condition when they brought him in, that was quite lucky."

"Oh?"

"They'd all been drinking at Bertha's. All three of them were pretty intoxicated," Greenwood said disapprovingly.

"Any particular reason for his fixation on Aruba?" McKernan asked.

"As a matter of fact, there is. After we got him sedated and settled down I talked to his buddies. It turns out our patient had himself quite a vacation there a few months before he shipped out to Mars. He spent a couple of weeks there soaking up the sun and the booze. It seems he met a woman there and had himself something of a fling. According to his friends, he was always talking about it to the point that they were getting sick of the whole topic."

"So you think that his obsessing over his vacation to Aruba triggered his episode?"

"You've been reading too much pop-psychology, Inspector. That's only part of the story."

"The way you're grinning, you've found something, haven't you?" McKernan queried. The problem of the psychotic epidemic had been intriguing Greenwood nearly as much as it had plagued the inspector.

"Yes, I have. Or at least I think I have. I took some blood when the patient was brought in. We ran the normal tox-screens, of course, which just turned up the alcohol, but I also ran a sample through the mass-spectrometer. It turned up something interesting."

"I can't stand the suspense, doc. What did you find?"

"Have you ever heard of something called Way Back?" Greenwood queried.

"No. Not that I can remember. I take it that it's some kind of drug?"

"That is something of an understatement. Way Back was one of the designer recreational pharmaceuticals that were so popular thirty or forty years back. It was also known as Playback or Memory Dust. It was really incredibly ingenious. Unlike opioids which just get the user high, Way Back functioned by interacting with the memory system of the brain. Essentially, it let the user relive some particular incident or event from their past, not a false memory, but the actual event. It's been described by users as reliving the past with almost perfect fidelity. Hence the name 'playback.' All the user would have to do is concentrate on the desired memory, ingest the drug, and it was as if they were reliving the whole incident all over again."

"It sounds pretty harmless. Was the drug addictive?"

"No, not in the usual sense. It doesn't create any physical cravings."

"So why haven't I run into it before? I've never heard of it or anything like it."

"In the first place, it was hideously expensive. The synthesis of the drug is extremely complex. The street price was in the range of a thousand dollars for a single dose, so it was mostly the plaything of the extremely rich or those involved in its manufacture. The second reason that it fell out of favor was that while under the influence, the user isn't aware of their surroundings. They actually think they are back wherever their memories take them. That can be awkward or dangerous, even back on Earth. Imagine thinking you're running across some field of wild flowers and getting run over by a bus because you were actually in the middle of a busy street."

"Or walking out an airlock thinking it's the door to the beach."

"Exactly. There was a third reason, too. It doesn't just let the user relive pleasant memories. A bit of mental indiscipline on the part of the user and they could end up reliving their worst nightmare. I understand that there were a number of 'bad trips' experienced by some people. In any case, the drug went out of favor, mostly because there were lots of more profitable drugs."

"So you think that your patient took some of this Way Back last night?"

"Not exactly. The exact formula for Way Back is something of a secret. I couldn't find it in the literature, but I contacted someone I know back on Earth who is a bit of an expert on these matters. He works for the U.N. Drug Enforcement Agency. He's actually their top scientist. Anyway, he looked at the mass spec results I got and said that they were similar, but not an exact match. He expected that the neurological reactions would be about the same, but that it had not been made using the same process that was used to synthesize Way Back."

"So, someone has come up with another process? Maybe something simpler or cheaper?"

"Well, this is where it get's interesting," Greenwood said. McKernan could tell that the doctor was getting excited by the topic. "As I said, the synthesis was very complex and expensive, which was one of the reasons Way Back never became popular. It turns out, though, that there are other ways to make complex organic molecules. The cells in living organisms make any number of them all the time and lots of plants and bacteria have had their genes modified to produce useful substances. One of the people working in that area at that time was an absolute genius at it. His name was Oliver Stanton. Some of his creations are still being used by the legitimate pharmaceutical industry. He was also something of a recreational drug user. He managed to modify the genome of a particular plant to produce the precursor of Way Back. Using that, it only takes a couple of simple steps to produce the actual drug, or at least something very much like it."

"So you think this Stanton is growing the drug?"

"Oh, no. According to my contact, Stanton brewed himself a massive amount of his concoction and took it all at once. He took a trip down memory lane and never came back. He's been stuck in an asylum for the insane for the last thirty years."

"So someone else is growing his plants?"

"Stanton supposedly destroyed them all before he took his trip. At least that's what the authorities claimed. There haven't been any reports of Way Back like drugs on Earth for the last thirty years."

"Until now."

"My contact says not. At least on Earth."

"Why would it show up on Mars but not on Earth?" McKernan asked. "That doesn't make sense. Why go to all the trouble of trying to smuggle it to Mars when you could make a lot more money selling it on Earth? Anything shipped here from Earth is checked pretty thoroughly."

"What if it's not being shipped from Earth?" Greenwood asked. "It might not be that easy to smuggle in the drug, but the seeds? People bring in seeds all the time to grow vegetables and herbs. I know you and Beth have got quite a garden going in your hut. So do I, for that matter. Almost everyone with space for a pot has something growing."

"You think someone is growing these plants and making Way Back here on Mars?"

"It makes as much sense an anything," Greenwood answered with a shrug.

CHAPTER 9

It was only a short walk down a corridor from Elena's office to the diner that served as the social hub of Junction 3. The original pneumatic hut had been replaced a few years earlier with a much larger building of fused silicon bricks, the ubiquitous building material for permanent structures on Mars. Junction 3 had started life as a way station on the newly built section of road, a place for travelers to stretch their legs and grab a bite to eat before moving on, an intersection point for the tracks leading off to a couple of mining camps and Station Alpha, a research facility, but it had evolved into a real community that consisted not only of the residents, but also those who roamed the neighboring Out There.

As Elena entered the diner she waved to the woman working behind the counter. The two had become fast friends as soon as Elena had been posted to Junction 3. At the time she and Jenny Huntley had been the only women living at the junction. Now there were more than a dozen female residents, but the two of them still remained close.

"Mind if I post this on the bulletin board?" Elena said, holding up one of her posters.

"Official business? Sure, go right ahead."

Elena tacked the poster up reusing one of the tacks that was already holding up a card from someone selling a used compressor.

"Can I get you lunch, Elena?"

"What's the special?"

"Bean soup and a ham on rye sandwich. Sorry, no cheese." The latter was something of a running joke. Vegetables were plentiful on Mars because they could be raised in small spaces. Chicken and eggs were becoming common, for the same reason. Pork products were less readily available, but could be found, but dairy products still had to be imported from Earth and therefore were rare and expensive. As Jenny's husband raised pigs, Junction 3 always had plenty of ham and bacon available.

"Sounds good," the constable responded.

"Where's Miguel? You've usually got him with you when you're not on patrol."

"I'm busy with a case, so Mike said he'd watch him at the shop. Miguel likes hanging around there, anyway. It's more exciting than watching me in the office."

"A case, eh? Is that what the poster's about?" Jenny asked curiously. Not much happened at Junction 3, so any bit of news was of interest.

"Yeah. I found an abandoned buggy and a body out past the 19 kilo marker as I was driving home last night. Turns out the registration number on the buggy is a phony. I'm trying to find out who the body belonged to. And where it is now."

"Didn't see you bring a buggy back. I figured you and Mike went out for something like that."

"The buggy wasn't there when I went back this morning. Neither was the body."

"That's pretty odd. I can see someone taking the buggy, but a body?"

"Yeah. I've got a real mystery on my hands. You haven't noticed a buggy with registration J-973 around have you?"

"I don't get outside much," Jenny replied.

"What about a stranger, maybe 180 centimeters? I'm not sure about hair color because he had his helmet on."

"That could describe half the men on Mars, Elena, but there hasn't been anybody new in here in months. Just the same old faces."

Elena had been hoping Jenny might have some idea who the dead man had been. Sooner or later just about everyone within a five hundred kilometer circle came to Junction 3 for supplies, to make a connection with the road train, or just to see another human face, and Jenny and the diner served as the hub of that small community.

Noting the disappointment in Elena's face, Jenny said, "You might ask Gus, over there. He notices everything." She nodded towards a man sitting at the counter enjoying the lunch special.

Elena knew Gus by sight, as she knew most of the couple of hundred people that lived within a day's drive of Junction 3. Gus, or Augustus Schwarz, was a geologist that ran surveys on contract for some of the mining operations. German by birth, he had a slight build, and stood just under average height. He was quiet, but had always struck the constable as having a good sense of humor.

"I couldn't help overhearing you ladies talk," Gus said in scarcely accented English. "I hope you don't mind?"

"Not at all," Elena responded, casually. "Do you remember seeing a buggy with registration J-973? Standard model, maybe four-five years old."

"Ja, maybe. A couple of months back I was doing a survey a little to the north-west of here. I saw a buggy heading north. I gave them a call on the radio, but I got no response. The number was J-9 something. It was a kilometer or more away and traveling at an angle, so I didn't get too good a look. Might have been the one you're looking for."

"Any idea who it was or where they were headed?"

"Sorry, no. I hadn't seen it before and I haven't seen it since. As far as I know there's not much up that way. Nobody I know of, at least. It's quite a bit to the west of Station Alpha, too, so I doubt it was anyone from there."

"Do you know of anyone else working up around there?" Elena asked.

"No. I'm afraid not."

"Well, thanks for your help, anyway, Gus."

"No problem. Sorry I couldn't be more sure."

Before the soup came, Mike wandered in from the shop with Miguel in tow, and Elena's focus turned to her son.

When Elena got back to her office she saw that there was a call waiting from Gaeretts on her computer. She called him back.

"Hi, Elena," Gaeretts said as he answered.

"Did you have any luck with the satellite imagery?"

"Sort of," Gaeretts replied. "None of the regular survey satellites were taking images over your area yesterday. Either they weren't overhead or they were busy looking at something else."

"That's too bad."

"Yeah. I did check around, though. Turns out that there's a met satellite that's doing a long term study of cloud cover. It's in a higher polar orbit and takes wider frame images. It covers the whole planet several times a day. It was overhead three times yesterday around 1000, 1330 and 1700. The latter was about the time you were there, wasn't it?"

"Yeah, just about."

"The trouble is," Gaeretts continued, "that the images, because they cover such a big area, are pretty low resolution. They can just barely pick up something the size of a buggy. I thought you'd find them interesting, though, so they should be in your in-box."

"I'll give them a look. Thanks, sergeant."

"Let me know if there's anything else I can do for you?"

"I will. Bye."

While Elena had been talking to Gaeretts, she noticed that a message had popped into her inbox. When she opened it, she saw that it was from Northern & Big Sky's safety officer. She hadn't expected a reply so quickly, but evidently Northern took the safety of their employees seriously. The message read:

We've done a quick check and all of our workers in the field are accounted for. Is there anything we should be aware of?

Well, Elena thought, it had been a good idea, but it had turned out to be a dead end. She sent a thank you in acknowledgement, and informed them that no further action was required.

Elena pulled up the first of the images Gaeretts had sent her on her screen, the one from 1000. Gaeretts had been right; the resolution of the image was pretty poor. She got out a map of the area and used it to find her bearings on the image, then expanded the portion where she had found the buggy until she reached the pixel limits. There was nothing there, or at least nothing that showed up in the image.

Disappointed, she took the last image and followed the same procedure. This time she was helped by the fact that the shadow cast by the buggy covered a larger area. There was something there, alright. It took up about half a dozen pixels on the image. It was hard to tell for sure, but it might be a buggy. There was only one, though.

She looked at the time stamp on the image. It was 1703. She knew from her radio log that she had found the buggy just after that. She'd called Mike at 1708 to tell him she'd be running late. That meant that her own buggy must have been just a few kilometers up the road from where she was looking. She backed out the image and slid the image to follow the road. She thought she spotted something. She expanded the image to maximum again. There it was, right in the middle of the road, the few darkened pixels that represented her own buggy. So the satellite had caught both her and the buggy by the body in the same image. At least she could prove now that she hadn't imagined the whole thing.

She noted the coordinates on the image of both her buggy and the one that she'd found. Returning to the first image, she checked the same coordinates, but there was nothing there. That left the middle image, the one that had been taken at 1330. There was an outcrop nearby that she could use as a reference mark. She got the alignment right and then looked at where she had spotted the buggy in the later image. The sun had been higher overhead, so the shadows weren't as pronounced, but if she expanded the image she could see a pair of darker pixels just where the buggy was in the later image, or at least she thought she could see it.

It still didn't tell her whose body it was she had found, but at least now she could show that there *had* been a buggy there, and maybe a body, too. And she knew that it hadn't been there at 1000 in the morning, had appeared a little after noon, and it had still been there when she found it just after 1700. And then it hadn't been there when she came back in the morning. So who had come to reclaim the body? And why?

She put the image and the coordinates in an e-mail and sent it off to Chief Inspector McKernan.

Chapter 10

As McKernan walked back across the Concourse towards his office he thought about what Greenwood had told him. The thought of a drug that allowed someone to get so lost in their past that they weren't aware of their surroundings was disturbing, but the facts seemed to fit with what he had been seeing with the epidemic of psychosis. What was more disturbing was that it seemed to be a purely Martian problem. If the drug were being imported from Earth, there might be some hope of intercepting it, if for no other reason than that all shipments from Earth were tightly controlled because of the high cost of transportation. But if the drug was being manufactured on Mars, the only hope of stopping it would be to discover where it was being made and by whom.

That might not prove an easy task. Mars was a big place. McKernan doubted that the drug was being manufactured in Mars City or even Hut Town. It would be too difficult to keep something like that a secret there. But there were plenty of places in the Out There where someone could operate without attracting attention. Greenwood had given him a copy of the report he had gotten from the U.N. Drug agency. Maybe there would be something in the report that would make his task easier.

The inspector had been so engrossed in his thoughts that he hadn't noticed what was happening on the Concourse. Normally, the Concourse was relatively empty.

Even at noon, people tended to move across it rather than linger.   Today, however, a temporary stage had been erected at one end of the big space and a crowd had gathered in front of it. McKernan stopped in his tracks and headed over to see what was going on.

Across the front of the stage a green banner had been draped with "The Future is Mars," the slogan of the green party, printed on it. A couple of P.A. speakers had been set up on either side and were being fed by a microphone that had been positioned in the middle of the stage. No one was speaking yet, but McKernan recognized a couple of leading activists from the Futurists waiting behind the stage. As he glanced around, he noted that there was someone with a camera getting ready to record the event.

For Mars, the crowd was impressive. There were few places on Mars where that many people could gather all at once, and large, empty spaces tended to make Martians nervous. For the most part, the people in the crowd were waiting calmly, seemingly drawn more by curiosity than anything else, but here and there the conversations were getting animated.

"Quite a show, isn't it?"

McKernan turned around to face his second in command, Gaeretts. Looking around he saw Ferris, one of his constables, hanging around on the fringes of the crowd.

"Did you know about this?" McKernan asked.

"Eddy Tokara came to me a couple of days ago to ask about getting a permit," the sergeant answered.

"And you didn't think to mention it to me?"

"I knew you were busy with this memory epidemic thing and the elections," Gaeretts replied.

McKernan was about to say something, but thought better of it. He gave his sergeant a lot of latitude to act as he saw fit and he'd never had cause to regret it.

"So what did you tell him?"

"What could I tell him? There's no official policy on public gatherings or permits, for that matter. I told him to go ahead, just make sure that he didn't block any of the exits. He seemed satisfied with that and went away."

McKernan just grunted. That, he thought, was part of the problem with the current situation, and why the upcoming negotiations on home rule were so important. No one in the U.N. Trust Authority cared anything about the day to day operations on Mars. All that really mattered back on Earth were the royalties that were extracted from the mining companies. There were, in effect, no laws other than those that governed the mining concessions. His own department was a law enforcement agency without a law code to enforce. He and his constables tried to use common sense, and for the most part that worked, but there was no mechanism in place to establish even the most basic rules. His department was only able to function because he had the support of the Trust Authority and the companies, but that situation could easily become unworkable. What would happen if the Pragmatists had chosen to hold a rally at the same time and place?

Gaeretts must have read his mind because he commented, "Tokara and Peterson got together and reached an agreement. The Greens rally today and the Reds rally on Friday. Sunday they meet to hold a debate."

"That seems reasonable," McKernan said. What he thought to himself, was that as long as people acted sensibly, things worked, but if they didn't—there'd be a problem and he'd have a mess on his hands to clean up.

His attention was drawn by someone getting up and introducing Tokara. The party spokesman got up on the stage and started in on a speech. Tokara was a good speaker. He could get right to the point and his arguments were coherent and reasoned, but McKernan had heard it all before. It would be great, he thought, if you could step outside without freezing or dying from lack of oxygen, but no matter what was done, it wasn't going to happen in his lifetime. What was more important was that people had title to the work they put into their homes and businesses and that there was some sort of legal structure behind all the activities of daily life. Though he was trying to be impartial, at heart he knew he was a Pragmatist.

He nudged Gaeretts and said, "I'm heading back to the office. If things get out of hand let me know."

The sergeant just nodded.

Settled back in his office, McKernan started to read the report that Greenwood had downloaded from his contact in the U.N. Drug Enforcement Agency. He noticed with interest that the file was marked "Distribution Restricted." The U.N. didn't have "Top Secret" or "Classified," but someone in the chain of command had decided that the information in the report was too sensitive to be freely disseminated.

The document began with a history of the drug. As with many abused drugs, Way Back had come out of research meant to heal. Originally, it had been seen as a treatment for Alzheimer's and other forms of dementia. Put simply, the drug was intended to facilitate the recall of memories. It had been successful, up to a point. At moderate dosages the effects of the drug were fleeting, minutes at most, which meant that its therapeutic uses were limited. At higher dosages, the effects were longer lasting, but the user stood the risk of getting caught in an endless loop of recall where the same event was replayed over and over again. This apparently was what had happened to Oliver Stanton.

Stanton had been a brilliant, if erratic researcher. On the verge of receiving his doctorate, he had been hired away from academia by a large pharmaceutical company where he had worked on the production of various medicines through the genetic modification of plants. He had evidently been quite successful at this for within several years he was the head of his own laboratory and basically allowed to work on whatever he wanted. He had become obsessed with the drug known popularly as Way Back. The report speculated that this was the result of his own mother having suffered from Alzheimer's.

As Greenwood had told him, Stanton had succeeded in breeding a plant that would produce a precursor of a drug very similar to Way Back, a substance that, with relatively few steps could be converted into the actual drug. Then Stanton's mother had died. The researcher had been overcome by the loss. In a fit of grief he had destroyed all his notes and the plants that he had modified and had then taken all of the drug that he had manufactured in one massive dose. He had been found by one of his assistants in an "unresponsive state" according to the report. He had never recovered and had been confined to a nursing home ever since. Stanton, in his last act, had apparently wiped out every trace of his research. Given the "unfortunate side-effects" the U.N. D.E.A. had recommended that information about Stanton's work on the drug be restricted. They had, as far as was known, evidently been successful. Way Back and related drugs had ceased to be a problem. The conventional production methods for the drug were far too expensive for it to be attractive to the illegal pharmaceutical trade.

Except that, from all the evidence McKernan had, it looked as if someone had succeeded in making Way Back or something similar on Mars. Now there were plenty of smart people on Mars, many of whom had the scientific training and access to the proper equipment to do something like that.   From time to time, one of these people would succeed in producing one or another of the simpler recreational drugs.   But, from what McKernan could glean from the report, the production of Way Back would likely be far beyond the abilities of anyone on Mars.   That was, unless they had access to some of Stanton's genetically modified plants to bypass the more difficult parts of the process.

The historical portion of the report was followed by several more technical sections.   One dealt with the clinical aspects of Way Back.   A lot of that was in jargon the McKernan didn't really understand, but the descriptions of the symptoms exhibited by subjects who had taken the drug matched those of the victims of the Martian epidemic.   As far as McKernan could tell, Dr. Greenwood was of the same opinion.

Another section covered the details of the process used to synthesize the drug.   This had so many formulas, tables, and charts that McKernan didn't even attempt to follow the description of the process.   A final addendum consisted of some speculations about Stanton's work.

McKernan was about to tackle these when he noticed the time.   Somehow, he had managed to spend an entire afternoon immersed in the report.   Beth would be expecting him home for dinner in less than twenty minutes.   He closed the file and headed home.

On his way through the Concourse he noted that the crowd had dispersed, apparently without a trace.   The stage had been dismantled and there weren't even signs of litter where the crowd had been.   One thing you could say about Martians, McKernan thought, was that they were neat.

CHAPTER 11

When she was back in her office after lunch, Elena thought about what Gus had said. He hadn't been sure about the number, but at the moment it was about the only lead she had to work with. She knew most of the people working in the area, that was part of her job, but her regular patrols were pretty much confined to the road. It was only when she got an emergency call that she ventured very far into the Out There. Given that the area assigned to her included everything within five hundred kilometers on either side of the road, that added up to a square a thousand kilometers on either side; one million square kilometers. There were plenty of areas in that territory that she'd never seen and probably never would.

She had a list of all the vehicles that were registered as working in that territory. She did a quick check, trying to find a match to the partial number that Gus had given her. She wasn't surprised when she didn't turn up any registrations that began J-9. At least, though, she could probably rule out the possibility that the buggy Gus had spotted was some unconnected one and not the vehicle that she was interested in.

On her computer she brought up a map of the area to the northwest of Junction 3. As Gus had said, there wasn't a lot going on up that way, at least officially. Of course, it was possible that the buggy Gus had spotted had been that of a wildcatter, but most of the independent prospectors made a habit of checking in regularly just so that someone would know where they were if they ran into trouble. Yet her contact list didn't show anyone currently working in that section. About the only activity even remotely in that area was a small base camp operated by Anglo-Martian, but that was almost too far to the west. Still, it couldn't hurt to give them a call.

Elena didn't have any trouble getting through to the Anglo-Martian camp. Anglo-Martian was a well-established outfit that didn't cut corners. Even for a small camp they usually set up relay towers for communications, so she didn't have to wait for a communications satellite to be in range.

She knew slightly the man who answered the phone. His name was Willem "Dutch" Van der Camp. He was an older man, which on Mars meant that he was over forty, tall and muscular, with cropped blonde hair that was starting to thin. Usually he was pretty affable, and this occasion was no exception.

"Constable Ortiz, to what do I owe the pleasure of your call?"

"Hi, Dutch. I'm looking for some information. We've gotten a report about a buggy that may have gotten itself into some trouble. I'm just calling on the chance that it was one of yours."

"All of our people are present and accounted for, so I don't think it was anyone from here," Dutch assured her.

"You don't have any buggies whose registration starts J-9, do you?"

"No. We only have four, and none of the registrations are anything like that. What's this about?"

Elena debated on how much she should tell him. She decided to err on the side of caution. "It's probably nothing. It's just that a prospector spotted a buggy he didn't recognize. It was quite a ways away, which is why he could only get a partial registration number. He tried to raise them, but they didn't respond. He didn't think much about it at the time, but decided later to mention it. The sighting was some hundred kilometers to the east of you, but you're the closest operation, so I just thought I'd give you a call to make sure it wasn't one of yours."

"No. It couldn't have been one of ours. Except for supply runs down to Junction 2 and back they all stick pretty close to camp. I'd know if any of my people had traveled that far east, and they haven't."

She didn't know if Van der Camp suspected there was more to her query than she had let on, but he didn't seem inclined to raise any questions of his own.

"Well, like I said, I was just checking. You haven't seen anyone else in your area that it might have been, have you?"

"No. As far as I know, we're pretty much all alone up here. The only person outside my crew that I've seen in a month was Gus Schwarz who spent the night a few weeks back."

Elena didn't know whether to be disappointed by the information or not. It just seemed to add to the mystery. "Well, thanks for the information, Dutch. Have a nice day."

"Sure thing. Say, Elena, are you all ready for the election?"

"As ready as I'll ever be, I guess."

"Sounds like there's going to be a regular party at Junction 3 that night."

"That's what people keep telling me. I know Jenny has been laying in extra supplies. Seems like everybody in the sector will be coming in to vote. What about you?"

"Oh, I'll be there. Wouldn't miss it for anything. There's a dozen of us here in camp that are eligible to vote, which is to say all of us, so we're going to pile into as many buggies as it takes and drive on down."

"You might want to plan on sleeping in your buggies, then. It's going to be pretty cramped here. From what people have been telling me, we might have three hundred or more show up to vote."

"It's sure a big deal, isn't it?" Dutch commented.

"That it is, Dutch. I'll be looking forward to seeing you."

"Well, good-bye, then. And say hello to Mike and little Miguel for me."

"I'll do that. Bye, and thanks again."

With the business of the body, Elena had nearly forgotten about the election until Dutch had brought it up. He had been right, though; it was a big deal, the first step on the road to home rule and independence for Mars. Of course, that's just what it was, a first step. The election would select the delegates for a constitutional convention which was supposed to come up with a document that would serve as the basis for self-government. After that, the U.N. Trust Authority and General Assembly would have their say in the matter. There was no guarantee that the constitution would be accepted. There had been promises made and broken before, some dating back even before she had come to Mars. But this time, things seemed different. There were a lot more people now who had chosen to make Mars their home and their future. It was the world that Miguel was going to grow up in. She just hoped it would be a one where he would have a chance to prosper.

Personally, she wasn't sure which side she took between the Reds and the Greens. On a practical level, most of the differences between them seem pretty minor. It was just as well that as an election official she was supposed to remain neutral.

In the meantime, though, she had a murder to solve, or at least the mystery of a death to deal with. If she was to believe Gus, and she had no reason to doubt him, someone was operating or at least active in, an area where no one was officially acknowledged to be working. Maybe what they were doing was innocent, but innocent people don't walk away with bodies and try to cover up the fact. But how was she going to find out what was going on? She couldn't just go and drive up where Gus had spotted the buggy, there was just too much territory to cover.

What she needed to do was narrow down the search area. She picked up her comm again and called Gaeretts.

"Elena, I've been expecting you to call," the sergeant said when he picked up.

"Oh?"

"I saw the photos and the note you sent the chief. Looks like you didn't imagine the whole business, after all."

Elena new Gaeretts well enough to know that he was just kidding and had never questioned what she'd seen.

"Yeah. But it's good to have some proof, even if it is only a few pixels."

"You didn't just call to gloat, though, did you?" the sergeant responded.

"No. I need some more satellite images."

"Of what? I got you everything from the time around when you found the body."

"I've got a hunch that something is going on somewhere in the area to the northwest of Junction 3, something that I think might be related to my body."

"Like what?"

"That's just it, sergeant, I don't know. That's why I want the photos."

"That's a mighty big area you're talking about, Elena."

"Yeah, I know. That's why I want the images to help me narrow it down."

"What exactly do you want?"

"Any images you can dig up from the last few months of the area around—" she gave him the coordinates that she had gotten from Gus. "Say in a square a hundred kilometers on a side. The higher the resolution, the better."

"You're asking for a lot, my girl." She would have resented the last from anyone else, but with Gaeretts, she could accept it.

"I know. But at this point I don't know what else to do. I don't have a body, I don't have the buggy. I don't even know who the guy was. All I have to go on is that somebody is up to something in that area and it seems that they don't want anyone else to know about it."

"It's going to take some time, Elena," Gaeretts said with a sigh, "but I'll see what I can do."

"Thanks. I'll be waiting."

After the call ended, Elena thought to herself, was she making too big a thing about this case? After all, there really wasn't any evidence that a crime had been committed. Everything indicated that the man, whoever he was, had just decided to open the faceplate of his surface suit. There had been no signs of foul play, no evidence that anyone else had been with him at the moment that he had died. Maybe it had just been a case of suicide. Maybe his partner or his friends had found the body afterwards and decided to take care of matters themselves. It was possible. Martians had the habit of taking care of things themselves, and you ran into some pretty odd characters in the Out There, people who had some strange notions as to what was or wasn't right.

Somehow, though, she didn't think that that was the case.

CHAPTER 12

It had been a good dinner. When Erik had first met Beth, she hadn't been much of a cook, particularly working under the conditions on Mars, but in the three years that she'd been sharing his place in Hut Town, she'd picked up a lot of new skills, cooking being one of them. Not that cooking was easy on Mars. Given the lower air pressure in the hut, a lot of meals had to be made in a pressure cooker, which had its limitations. The choice of ingredients could be limited, as well. A lot of what they ate, they either grew themselves or traded for with others. Most protein had to be imported from Earth which meant that it was expensive and sometimes hard to come by. To be a good cook on Mars you had to develop a talent for using what was on hand and be willing to make substitutions on the fly.

Tonight's dinner had been a bean casserole, leavened with tomatoes and zucchini, with a little bit of chicken and bacon to add substance and flavor. The wine they had washed it down with had come out of a pouch because it was cheaper to ship it to Mars that way than in a bottle. It had been a good wine, though, a syrah-grenache blend from Australia. When the major expense of a wine was based on its mass and volume it didn't make sense to skimp on quality.

The dinner table conversation had been dominated by small talk. They'd both learned that it was better that way.

The minutia of everyday life, the patients that Beth had seen at the hospital, the cases that Erik worked on, those were safe topics. The future, not so much.

As they were clearing the table afterwards, Erik asked, "Would you mind cleaning up on your own. I've got some stuff from work that I need to go over."

"No, you go ahead," Beth answered. "There's not that much to clean up, anyhow." She knew that Erik, despite his responsibilities, did more than his share of the household chores. They both had erratic schedules and had adjusted their lives to accommodate them.

Erik moved to the part of the hut they called the living room and sat down on a couch that had been fabricated out of metal tubing and seats scavenged from an old buggy. As with most of the furnishings in the hut, it didn't look like much, but it was comfortable.

After Beth had finished cleaning up in the kitchen she poured herself another glass of wine and went to sit next to the inspector.

"What are you reading?"

"It's a report from the U.N. Drug agency," Erik said distractedly.

"Does this have anything to do with the psychotic cases we've been seeing lately?" Beth asked. As one of the small staff of doctors, she had had firsthand experience with the epidemic.

"Yes. Greenwood has this idea that the problem is being caused by a synthetic drug. There was a similar sort of problem with a drug on Earth some years back. It was called Way Back, Playback, or Memory Dust. This is the report that was issued at the time."

"I don't remember ever reading about it," Beth said, curious.

"It was never a big problem. The original drug was much too expensive to produce to be of interest to the criminal element. The manufacturing process was just too complex. At the time it was mainly a curiosity. Except that a guy named Stanton managed to come up with a shortcut in making it. He manipulated a plant to produce a precursor to the drug that cut out a lot of the more complicated and expensive steps in the synthesis. Fortunately, he took some of the drug himself and has been in an institution ever since. It had been thought that all of the details of his experiments had been destroyed."

"But I take it you have your doubts?"

"What we've been seeing here on Mars matches the symptoms as described in the report. That makes me think that either someone had access to Stanton's work or was able to recreate it."

"And you think this drug is being synthesized here on Mars?"

"That would be my guess. We keep a pretty close eye on what comes in, and there are much more lucrative things that could be smuggled in from Earth. Why go to all the trouble shipping in something expensive when you could bring in something cheap? It's more likely that someone has brought in the seeds of this modified plant and is growing them and making the drug here."

"Here in Mars City?"

"That's what I'm trying to figure out. Unfortunately, I don't have a background in organic chemistry and this report gets pretty technical. What I'd like to know is how many of these plants would they have to grow and what sort of equipment would be needed to complete the synthesis?"

"Would you like me to take a look at it?" Beth asked.

"Would you?" Erik agreed with a smile. He handed over the tablet that he'd been reading the report on.

Beth started reading, and was soon deep in concentration. Rather than disturb her, Erik got up and poured himself another glass of wine. He had almost finished it before Beth set the tablet down on the table next to her.

"It's been awhile since I've done much biochemistry, not since pre-med, really, but I think I have some idea of what the process entails. If I understand things correctly it would take a lot of plants to produce enough seeds to make the kind of quantities that we're talking about. A lot more than could be grown in someone's living quarters."

"You mean, it would take someplace like an abandoned hut in Hut Town?" Erik knew that there were unused huts available for the taking at the far end of Hut Town.

"No, I mean someplace much bigger than that. I'd guess that it would take hundreds, maybe thousands of square meters."

"About the size of a football field. That big of an operation would be pretty hard to hide anywhere in the neighborhood of Mars City," Erik commented, more to himself than to Beth.

"Yes, unless they could camouflage it as some sort of farming operation."

"You said they. You think that we're talking about more than one person?"

"It would take a lot of labor to tend the number of plants needed."

"What about the processing equipment? What sort of facility would that be?"

"Technically, it's nothing particularly special. There would have to be some sort of apparatus to crush the seeds and then refine the results. That would require distillation and then vacuum evaporation. It would be kind of specialized equipment to handle the volumes involved, but nothing that somebody who was clever with their hands couldn't make if they had the tools and material. Let's face it, Martians have become pretty good at making do with what they've got at hand."

"So let me get this straight in my mind. You're saying that it would take a lot of area, say maybe a hectare of plants and some sort of fairly sophisticated chemical plant to produce the drug?"

"Yes, if you extrapolate from the information in this report," Beth confirmed. "Given the number of cases that have been reported, and assuming that there are a lot more cases where the user hasn't attracted attention, I'd have to say that we're talking about a thousand doses at a minimum. My guess is that it would take around a hundred plants per dose."

"That's a lot more than you could hide even in the back end of Hut Town."

"Yes. I think you're right about that."

Later McKernan was still thinking about the implications of their discussion as they lay in bed when Beth asked, "Erik, do you ever think about the future?"

"What do you mean?" He and Beth had had this discussion before, and it had never gone well.

"What's going to happen if this home rule thing really goes through?"

"I haven't given it much thought. I expect that things won't really change all that much."

"But what about us, Erik? What will it mean for us personally?"

"For us? I'm not sure that it will have much of an effect. Anyway, whatever happens is going to take a long time. Maybe years."

"But we both work for the Trust Authority. If some sort of new government is formed, where does that put us? Will we still have jobs?"

"There's still going to be a need for doctors. And I would hope for policemen, too."

"But what I'm asking is will they need *us?*"

"I wouldn't worry. There aren't that many doctors willing to live on Mars. Certainly not with your experience. Besides, Greenwood would back you, and I can't see them getting rid of him. As for me, well, even if they don't want me as a policeman I can always find something to do. I can still be a pilot if need be."

"But, is it possible that we'd have to go back to Earth?"

Listening to her, Erik wasn't sure whether Beth was afraid of that possibility or was welcoming it. She had never been as committed to a life on Mars as he had. For her, it had always been a temporary assignment that had just been dragged out and extended. If she did go back, would she expect him to follow? Or, if he chose to stay, even without a job, would she stay with him?

"I don't know the answer to that?" Erik said.

CHAPTER 13

McKernan had told Elena that she could call in someone to cover her for her patrols if she thought she needed the time to pursue the case, but there hadn't seemed to be anything requiring her immediate attention, so she had decided on making her regular Thursday morning drive out to Junction 4. Of course, it was Thursday only on Mars. With a day that was almost forty minutes longer than Earth's, no pretense was made to synchronize dates, weeks or months to those of the home planet. Officially, Mars ran on Greenwich Mean Time, but as that was hopelessly out of step with the reality on the ground, it was pretty much ignored except when communicating with Earth. It did make it hard to keep track of holidays like Christmas, but, then, that was what computers were for.

Elena had made breakfast for Mike and Miguel, and said her good-byes, knowing that she'd be home in time for dinner the next day. As always, Mike had walked her through the check-out of her surface suit. They both knew that she was more than capable of handling that on her own, but Elena didn't mind. She liked the fact that she had someone that cared for her, and it was ten shared minutes when they could be intimate if not physically close. She had waved back at him when she was outside the airlock and then climbed into her buggy.

Elena had made the run to Junction 4 so many times that she probably could have done it in her sleep. Not that the constable wasn't alert. Losing focus was a sure way to get yourself killed on Mars. But one of the reasons that she had decided to make the patrol was that it would give her plenty of time to think.

And she had plenty of things to think over. She still didn't have much to go on: a bogus ID number for the buggy, a sighting of what might or might not have been the buggy she had found, vague reports of something going on somewhere in a vast expanse of the Out There. She still didn't have a name for the man she had found dead. She certainly didn't have a body. If she didn't come up with some more evidence, her case might end up as just one of those Martian mysteries that in ten years would become a legend. It wasn't exactly the way she wanted the first real case that she handled on her own to end up.

Maybe something would turn up in the imagery Gaeretts was digging up for her. Right now that was about her only hope of solving the case. But how much of a trace would two men leave on Mars? She knew that there had to have been at least two of them, the one who had died and whoever it was that had taken him away. More likely, there had to have been at least three of them, because someone would have had to have driven the dead man's buggy away. They must have left some sign of their activities. The thin atmosphere of Mars took a long time to wear tracks away. You could still find some of the trails left by the original unmanned rovers if you knew where to look. The problem, though, would be picking out the tracks you were interested in. After thirty years of prospectors and surveyors churning up the surface, there were plenty of tracks around to confuse things.

The section of the Road that ran from Junction 3 to Junction 4 wasn't nearly as well traveled as that which she had driven earlier in the week. Traffic tended to get heavier the closer you got to Mars City and Junction 3 was the confluence for a number of side roads that ran to the science base at Station Alpha and several mining operations. The terrain was more irregular, too, and the road had more twists and turns to it as it avoided obstacles that had been too big to plow over.

By the time Elena pulled over for lunch just past noon she hadn't passed a single vehicle. That wasn't unusual. You could fit a lot of traffic into five hundred kilometers without any of them being in sight of each other. Most people, if they were traveling the road, would set out early in the morning so that they could travel all the way to the next stop in daylight. If Elena was going to run into anyone going the other way it would probably happen in the next hour or two.

The buggy carried the usual assortment of ready to eat meals, but Jenny, who ran the road station and restaurant at Junction 3, made it a practice to pack her a lunch for the outbound leg of her patrols. The contents tended to be a surprise, depending on what was plentiful at the moment on the farm that her husband ran on land adjacent to the junction, but that was part of their charm.

Elena opened up the container full of anticipation. She was in luck. Jenny had been experimenting lately with making tortillas from home grown corn. She'd used one as a wrap around romaine lettuce and diced chicken covered in a tomato and pepper salsa. Jenny had thrown in a few carrots and stalks of celery as well. Elena thought that all she needed would be a cold beer to wash it down, but she knew she'd have to settle for some powdered drink mix and water from the buggy's tank.

Elena warmed the wrap in the buggy's microwave. Jenny had included some hot peppers in the salsa and the first bite reminded Elena of growing up in Brownsville. It had been a long time since she'd been back. Two years at Luna base with the Air Force, and then four years on Mars. She missed it sometimes, but she knew that she was never going back, not with Mike and Miguel here on Mars.

While she ate, she brought up the few photos she'd taken of the body the evening she'd found it. There was one of the face; not that that was much use. Decompression had distorted the features, and there was only so much that could be made out through the opening of the faceplate. About all that could be said was that the victim had been male, Caucasian, and probably somewhere between thirty and forty-five, give or take a few years. Elena knew that that described about two thirds of the population on Mars.

A bright idea came to her. She brought up a full length image of the body. Helmets were all pretty much a standard size, at least on the outside. Using that as a scale factor, Elena made an estimate of the body's height. It was pretty crude, the legs had been bent slightly, and the torso hadn't been completely straight, but as far as she could tell the mystery man had been just under a hundred and eighty centimeters, or about six feet even, give or take a couple of inches. It didn't look as if he had been overly plump, either.

So what did that leave her with for a description? A thirtyish white guy of average height or maybe slightly taller, and medium build. That narrowed it down to only about half of the people on Mars. It was something, though.

She'd pulled off the road near one of the relay towers, so she had no trouble completing a call to Sgt. Gaeretts.

"Hi, Elena. How's your mystery?"

"About the same. But I do have some information I'd like you to check on for me. I've worked up a rough description from the images I took when I found the body.

It's only an estimate, but I thought maybe you could check it against any reports of missing men." She read him the description she'd come up with.

"He didn't by any chance have a tattoo on his face or a wooden leg? That would make it easier," Gaeretts joked.

"Not that I could tell. I wasn't trying to ID him at the time."

"I'll give it a shot, Elena, but not too many people go missing on Mars. Not unless they do it on purpose, and those tend not to get reported."

"It's the best I've got at the moment. How are you doing on getting those satellite images I asked you for?"

"I've got a bunch of them. Too many, but I've kind of sorted out the ones that wouldn't do you any good. I'll send them out to you. Where are you? Junction 3?"

"No, I'm on my way to 4. I decided I might as well make my regular patrol."

"That will make Kaminski happy. I'll send the data packet along to Junction 4 so that it's waiting there when you get there tonight."

"Thanks, Sarge. I'll get in touch if I think of anything else. Let the Inspector know what I'm doing."

"OK. Bye."

Some forty-five minutes after her lunch break had ended Elena came across her first traffic of the day, a buggy towing a trailer heading the other way on the road. She pulled up and waited, and as the other vehicle drew abreast, it too stopped in the road. Given the emptiness of Mars, this wasn't unusual behavior. Most people in the Out There were more than eager to stop and chat when they ran across someone. Elena recognized the logo on the side of the buggy indicating that it belonged to Fukashima Rare Earths, one of the mining companies operating on Mars.

A cheerful "Hi, Elena, how goes it?" came out of the line-of-sight radio.

"That you Hiro? Is Ito with you?"

"Hi, Erena." Hiro's English was pretty good due to his having gone to the University of Wisconsin. Ito's was not as good, but he made up for it with friendliness.

"What are you guys up to?" Elena asked.

"They've got us running a bunch of samples in for assay," Hiro replied. "Going to have us a high time in the big city." Elena took that to mean Mars City, which was about the only place that qualified as a "city" on Mars.

"That's a long haul. Don't drive too long at a stretch."

"Oh, we'll probably stop a few hours at Junction 3, then drive through to 1 before catching some zees. We want to be fresh when we get to town."

"Just be careful."

"We will be, Mama Elena."

"There is something maybe you could help me with, Hiro. Have you ever run across a buggy with the registration J-973?"

"This about that body you found, Elena?"

"You heard about that, Hiro?"

"News travels fast when there's no other news."

"Yeah. That was the buggy he was driving," Elena commented.

"I don't think so. Not that I remember. What about you, Ito?"

A couple of sentences in Japanese came over the radio.

"Ito says that he remembers a buggy with the number I-978. He didn't recognize it and it didn't have a company logo on it."

"Where was this?"

There was some more discussion in Japanese, then, "Oh, a couple of months ago, maybe a little more. Up north of here. Ito's got a pretty good memory for numbers, so he's pretty sure about the registration."

"And you don't know who it was?"

"No. I didn't think anyone was working up in that area."

"So you don't know of any prospectors or wildcatters operating to the north?"

"Not that I've run across. Though, now that you ask, we've been running across tracks while running survey's up in that area. No way to tell how old they were, but they seemed fresh. Probably from the last year or so."

"One buggy, or two?"

"Couldn't say. One track looks pretty much like another. Except, one time they seemed to be towing a trailer with a heavy load."

"Do you remember where exactly this was?"

There was another exchange in Japanese. "No, sorry Elena. I can't remember and Ito doesn't either."

"Well, thanks any way. I'll let you guys get on your way. Have fun in Mars City."

"Thanks, Elena. We'll be back in time for the election. See you at Jenny's."

Elena said, "Bye" as the other buggy took off. What Hiro had had to say had been interesting. It wouldn't take much to change a registration of I-978 to J-973. That was something else to have Gaeretts check out. And, combined with what Gus had said, it looked to Elena as if something was going on to the north. The question was, where?

CHAPTER 14

In the morning, as usual, the first thing McKernan did after entering the office was ask Gaeretts if anything of note had happened during the night.

"The usual," Gaeretts replied laconically. A couple of fights out in Hut Town. Nothing serious. The participants were all too drunk to do much damage. The only injury was a black eye. They're in the cooler now, but I was going to let them go after they've sobered up."

"Quiet evening, then?"

"We did have an altercation of a political nature." From the smile on the sergeant's face, it was clear that he had a story to tell.

"Oh?" McKernan replied.

"A couple of science types got into it on the concourse. There was some pushing and shoving and a punch was thrown," Gaeretts answered. "Not that it landed, mind you."

"Any idea which one of them started it?"

"Hard to say. Witnesses statements vary depending on party affiliation. From what I was able to gather, the two had been discussing matters more or less calmly and then things just escalated."

"How did it end?" McKernan asked.

"Ferris managed to break it up before it got serious. He took down their names and told them to go home. They didn't give him any trouble after that. I was passing by after my dinner break just as it was ended and helped him take statements from witnesses. As I said, they tended to be biased depending on which party the witness belonged to."

"I'd like to put a brake on this kind of thing before it gets out of hand," McKernan said. "We've less than two weeks until the election, and in the mean time I'd like things to remain peaceful. See if you can arrange a lunch meeting with Tokara and Peterson."

"I'll see what I can do," Gaeretts answered.

"Anything else I need to know about?"

"Not that I know of."

"Have you heard from Elena?"

"She's been pestering me for imagery of the area to the northwest of Junction 3. She seems to think there might be something going on up there that's related to her disappearing body."

The inspector thought about it for a moment. "She may be right. Give her any help you can."

"You don't think that maybe this business is too much for her?" Gaeretts asked. "After all, it's her first time handling a case on her own, and this one seems more complicated than most."

"Every detective has a first case. Even I did. Elena can take care of herself. She's smart and has as much experience as anybody. Besides, there really isn't anyone to spare to help her out, is there?"

"No," the sergeant acknowledged.

"Well, keep me informed. And you might let Kaminski know he should be ready to back her up if she needs it. He's the closest, isn't he?"

"Yeah, but it would take him the better part of a day to get there."

"There are other people she can count on. Mike, for one. Just tell her to be careful and not to go charging in without checking with me first."

"Yes, sir."

"Good. I've got some things to look into this morning, but I should be back before noon for the meeting."

McKernan had been thinking over what Beth had told him last night after reading the report on Way Back. They'd come up with a list of the equipment that would be needed to manufacture the drug. None of it was the sort of thing that was readily available on Mars, but most of items could have been cobbled together by anyone with good mechanical skills. Mars had plenty of those kinds of people, bright, knowledgeable, and with hands on skills. But no matter how good they were, they'd need the raw materials and parts, and there weren't a lot of places to get them. Given shipping costs, the companies kept tight control of their inventories and he couldn't remember any of them reporting losses of that kind of material. That pretty much meant they would have had to have used the scrap and salvage market to furnish what they needed.

The most likely scrap dealer was in Hut Town, out towards the end of Corridor D. Everyone in Hut Town went there when they needed something, including McKernan.

As McKernan made is way out Corridor D, he noticed how much it had changed since he had first arrived on Mars. Fewer of the huts were abandoned and more of them were housing independent businesses. Even without a currency, Mars was developing its own internal economy despite the lack of encouragement from the Trust Authority.

His destination was pretty obvious. There was a big sign reading "The Hardware Store," hanging right above the air lock. Unlike most of the signs in Hut Town, this was a professional looking one on a piece of sheet metal, with careful lettering and drawings of a wrench and a hammer flanking the words. The story was that it had been painted by someone in exchange for a heater core. The story was probably true.

Inside, the hut ran back for fifty meters. The middle of hut was occupied by rows of shelving full of bins of plumbing fittings, electrical parts, motors, and just about anything else one could imagine. One side wall was dominated by tools of various kinds, from simple hand tools like wrenches and screwdrivers, to complex machine tools. The other side had lengths of piping, channel stock, angle brackets, and plastic and metal sheet goods. The one thing that all of it had in common, was that none of it was new. It had all been salvaged or scrapped, or rebuilt or restored. McKernan knew, too, that in addition to the sales hut, the owner had two or three more huts where excess inventory was stored.

At the entry to the hut was the sales counter where the proprietor could keep an eye on the airlock. The front of the counter was covered with price lists for some of the more common items. At one end of the counter was an old-fashioned balance scale. This was used when bartering for small pieces of hardware. If you didn't have the right size screw or nut or fitting, you could exchange whatever you had for whatever size you needed on a gram for gram basis with an allowance factor factored in when the materials were of different metals.

The proprietor looked up as McKernan walked through the airlock.

"What can I do for you inspector? I'm running a special on stainless steel tubing right now. Ten, twenty, and twenty-five millimeter inner diameter, assorted lengths. Or maybe some plastic panels, five mills thick."

"I'm looking for some information, Jerry" McKernan responded.

"That will be in aisle 5. Next to the batteries." The proprietor saw that his joke had fallen flat. "Sorry, I guess that line is as old as the hills. What kind of information are you looking for?"

"I'm looking for someone who might have acquired some specialized equipment in connection with a case. I've got a list of what I'm interested in right here." He pulled a piece of paper out of his pocket and slid it across the counter.

"I've got a lot of things, Inspector, but I don't think I've got most of what's on that list."

"I didn't thing you would. Probably no one on Mars does. But I think the people I'm looking for probably were smart enough to build their own if they could get their hands on the parts. That's why I came to you. You've got plenty of parts."

"Let me take a look at that list again," Jerry said. He studied it for a bit. "How much of this stuff do you think they would have needed?"

"Quite a bit of it. We're talking about a commercial operation, not someone putting something together in the back of their hut."

"Well, I get a lot of people coming in here, you know, they want one specific thing, a particular pump, a special fitting or coupler, a certain kind of circuit board, that kind of thing. Only a few of my customers come in for quantity, and most of them I know because I've dealt with them for years. But I remember dealing with a couple of fellows oh it must have been six months or so ago. They came in three or four times over the span of maybe a month. They bought a bunch of stuff, stainless steel plumbing, heat exchangers, pumps. Took it out the back airlock and loaded it onto a trailer hitched to a buggy. Does that sound what you're looking for?"

"It might be," McKernan responded. "The timing would be about right."

"I figured that they might be planning on setting up some kind of farming operation."

"Oh? What made you think that?"

"Well, one of the things they bought was grow lights. A lot of them. Nearly cleaned me out."

McKernan understood why Jerry thought they might be farmers. The solar intensity on Mars was a lot less than on Earth. Most plants required supplemental illumination to do well. He had a couple of grow lights himself for the plants he raised in the back of his hut.

"You don't happen to remember their names, do you?"

"I don't usually ask a lot of questions. Not unless someone is trying to sell me a lot of stuff or the deal looks fishy."

"So you don't know who these guys were?"

"I didn't say that, Inspector. Like I said, these two guys bought a lot of stuff. They'd brought some salvage in for trade, but it wasn't nearly enough to cover what they bought. They paid for a lot of it in company exchange script. Half a dozen different companies, but that's not unusual. Most people carry around at least a few companies' script."

Without an official currency, the coupons companies issued to their employees for use in the company stores served as a de facto replacement. Independent merchants would accept the coupons for goods and services and either redeem them themselves at the stores or barter them for things they needed. Technically it was against the regulations, but the companies mostly turned a blind eye to the practice as it was the only way to make things work. The problem was that the coupons were anonymous.

"That doesn't do me much good, I'm afraid," McKernan said.

"Hold your horses, Inspector. I said they paid for a lot of it using script, but they still came up short. So they paid for the rest of it in shipping allowances."

Most of the companies and the Trust Authority paid part of their employee's salaries in shipping allowances, which covered the cost of shipping so many kilograms from Earth. McKernan, had a five kilogram allowance an Earth month from the Trust Authority. Most shipping allowances went towards luxury items like alcohol or spices or other things that weren't readily available on Mars. The important thing was that shipping allowances were traceable back to the person to whom they were issued.

"Don't tell me you don't keep a record of those," Mckernan commented.

"I should hope I do, Inspector. Just give me a moment to check."

He spent a few minutes playing with a computer behind the counter.

"Here it is, Inspector. I've got two names for you. Frederick Jackson and Ian Bates."

McKernan scribbled the names down on the list of equipment.

"Do you remember anything else about these guys?"

"Not particularly. They were youngish, maybe mid to late twenties. I got the impression that they were technical types, not just hired muscle. One of them seemed to know a lot about chemical engineering. The other was more of a mechanical systems type. I can't remember which was which."

"And they never said what they were going to do with all this stuff they bought?"

"No, but then I didn't ask a lot of questions. It was mostly them saying they needed something and me going to fetch it, if you know what I mean."

"Did they say where they were going with it?"

"Sorry, no. But from the amount of wear on the buggy, it must be someplace way out in the Out There."

"Well, thanks for the help, Jerry. If you remember anything else about these guys let me know, won't you?"

"Sure thing, Inspector. If you don't mind my asking, is this something important? They didn't seem like bad kids, you know."

"It might be, Jerry. It might be."

It was almost noon when McKernan got back to the station.

"Tokara and Peterson are waiting for you in the conference room," Gaeretts said as he walked in the door.

The conference room was a cubicle just big enough for a table and a few chairs. Tokara was sitting on one side of the table, Peterson on the other. There didn't seem to be any particular animosity between them. McKernan noticed with approval that Gaeretts had thought to order in some sandwiches from one of the food carts on the Concourse.

"Thank you for coming, gentlemen," McKernan said taking a chair at the end of the table.

"What exactly is this about, Inspector?" Tokara asked trying to sound indignant.

"You've probably figured that out, already, but there was an incident on the Concourse last night. One of my constables stepped in before it got serious, but this is the second such incident that's come to my attention in the past few days."

"Just what kind of incident are you talking about?" This time it was Peterson who asked the question.

"I'm talking about a physical altercation between partisans of your respective parties."

"I'd hardly call it an altercation," Tokara broke in.

"Then you know what I am referring to?" McKernan queried. Both men nodded.

"Well, the discussion may have gotten a little heated," Peterson admitted.

"Throwing a punch is more than a discussion," McKernan objected.

"Just what is it you want us to do, Inspector?" Tokara asked.

"I want each of you to inform your party members that political violence of any sort will not be tolerated. Anyone who is caught participating in that kind of thing may find themselves on the next ship back to Earth."

"You can't do that, Inspector!" Peterson said emphatically.

"Until such time as home rule is established, I can. And I will! Do I make myself clear?"

There were sounds of grudging assent from both sides of the table.

"Good. Now you know I am as much in favor of home rule as either of you gentlemen," McKernan said, trying to mollify the two party leaders. "I think we can all agree that it is time for Mars to be given a say in what happens here, which is why it's important that this election goes off without a hitch."

Again there was agreement.

"I suggest then that we have lunch and discuss the plans for election day."

CHAPTER 15

It was after 1800 when Elena finally pulled into Junction 4. The way station was a lot smaller place than Junction 3, consisting of only a few huts buried under a half meter of sand as shielding against radiation. The permanent population numbered only about a dozen, most of which worked for the land-train concession. It was a place where travelers could get food, water, air, and fuel and find a corner to sleep in for the night, but that was about the extent of it.

After Elena had shut down her buggy she put on her surface suit and walked over to the main hut. The airlock opened into a combination locker and changing room. There weren't separate areas for men and women. Mars wasn't big on modesty in general, particularly this deep in the Out There where the population was overwhelmingly male. About the only accommodation a small station like Junction 4 offered to modesty was a corner of the room shielded by a shoulder high partition. After vacuuming the dust off her suit, Elena didn't bother to go behind it. She changed into leggings and a sweater and stowed her suit in one of the empty lockers. Despite the name, there wasn't a lock on the locker door. Junction 4 was too small for strangers. Besides, there probably wasn't anyone within a hundred kilometers that could have fit into her surface suit.

Beyond the changing room was a space that ran the width of the hut that served as a combination waiting area, dining room, and overflow sleeping area for when the land train stopped. There were only three people in the room. A couple of men in company coveralls were sitting together at a table. They looked like miners, and were probably waiting for the train which was due sometime during the night if it was running on schedule. The third man, who was clearing plates from the table, was Lewis Jones, the station master.

When Jones spotted her he called out, "There's still some soup hot in the kitchen, Elena. Creamy potato. Made it myself with real condensed milk. Hot coffee, too."

"Sounds good, Lew." It wasn't up to the standards of Jenny's cooking, but after a day of driving it sounded good enough.

"How's little Miguel doing?" the station master asked.

She knew she should be tired of the fact that Miguel and the state of his health had always to be a prime topic of conversation, but Elena didn't mind. After all, there wasn't much else to talk about, certainly not the weather. Besides, for old timers like Jones, Miguel, and the few other kids like him, represented the future of Mars.

"He's doing just fine, Lew. I think he takes after his father more every day."

"Good to hear. You should bring him with you on patrol one of these days. Oh, there was a data packet that arrived for you from Sgt. Gaeretts. A big one. I shunted it off to the server, so you can access it in your office."

"Thanks. I was expecting it."

"Something to do with that body you found?" Jones asked, obviously curious.

"Maybe," Elena replied noncommittally. When she noticed the disappointment of the station master she added, "I'm trying to figure out where the body came from—and where it went."

"Pretty odd, that. I mean the body disappearing in the middle of the night like that."

Jones had a point, Elena thought. Temperatures plummeted pretty rapidly once the sun set, limiting the time one could spend outside even in a good surface suit with the heaters running full on. Working at night increased the likelihood of things going wrong, and when something went wrong on Mars it most often was fatally.

"Yeah, whoever moved it must have really wanted to keep the victim's identity secret. No other reason I can think of. After all, they had to have known from the fact that it was covered that the body had been found by someone else."

"Seems you've got a real mystery on your hands, Elena," Jones said shaking his head.

"Yeah, I sure do. Say, you wouldn't have any ideas about anybody unusual who's been working to the north of here, would you?"

"You think they might be connected to your body?"

Elena wasn't sure that she liked the fact that everybody seemed to be referring to it as her body.

"Maybe. I ran into Hiro and Ito on the way here today, and they said something about seeing a buggy that might have belonged to the dead man running up that way. Gus thought he'd seen someone, too, but none of them had a chance to get close enough to have any idea as to who it was."

"I'm afraid I can't help you. Let's face it, any stranger around here would stick out like a sore thumb, but all I've seen in the last few months are the same old faces. Yours is about the freshest, and that's because you only show up once a week."

"Well if you see anyone new or hear anything, let me know."

"Sure thing, Elena."

"Thanks, Lew. And I'd appreciate it if you could bring that soup and a cup of that coffee to me in the office."

"Sure thing, Elena," Jones replied.

The security office at Junction 4 wasn't much more than a three by four meter cubicle off of the main hall of the station hut. The furnishings consisted of a table, a chair, a cot, and not much else, but for Elena it was home one night a week. She kept a change of clothes, a spare toothbrush and a few other things in a storage bin for emergencies. Kaminsky, who drove patrol on the section of road from Junction 5 to Junction 4, had a storage bin with his own personal items, but their schedules were such that they rarely had to worry about who got the cot.

Elena had just finished changing into a pair of warm slippers when Jones brought in a large bowl of soup and a coffee mug.

"Thanks, Lew. Looks good. Anything exciting happen lately?"

"At Junction 4? Not in my lifetime. The only thing exciting to happen is the election, and it sounds like everyone is heading to Jenny's for that. I have a feeling I'm going to be here by my lonesome for the big event."

"Sorry about that," Elena commiserated.

"Hell, I'd head there myself except that someone has to man the station. Well, I'll let you eat in peace. I imagine you're in a hurry to look at that data packet."

"Thanks, Lew."

After Jones had left, Elena called Gaeretts to check in using the office computer. A few years earlier, a fiberoptic cable had been run the then extent length of the road with drops at each of the junctions out to Five as well as the cell towers along the road. This provided enough bandwidth to support a full video connection in both directions. After a few moments, the sergeant's image appeared on the screen.

"I see you made it to Four," Gaeretts said laconically.

"Yeah, I just got in a few minutes ago," Elena commented

"Anything to report?"

"Not much. Your data packet arrived intact. I was just getting ready to go through it."

"Well, don't sit up all night looking at it. You've got a long drive ahead of you tomorrow." Despite his gruff manner, Gaeretts was solicitous of his one female patrol constable.

"I won't, sergeant. One thing, though. I ran into Hiro and Ito on the road today. They mentioned coming across a buggy with the registration of I-978 up north of the road. It wasn't sporting any company logo."

"So?"

"So it wouldn't take more than a little paint to make I-978 into J-973. I thought that maybe you could trace the registration."

"You think this buggy the Japs spotted was being driven by your missing body?"

"Either that or the people who made the body go missing," Elena responded.

"It's worth checking out," Gaeretts conceded. "I'll look into it."

"Thanks."

"Anything else?"

"Nope. I'm about to dig into a bowl of soup and start looking at pictures."

"OK. Take care. And don't stay up too late."

"Bye."

Elena cut the connection and opened up the data packet from Gaeretts while she ate. She could see that it was going to take a long time. Despite the sergeant's editing, there were more than a thousand images in the data packet he had sent her.

CHAPTER 16

After his initial declaration, McKernan thought that the lunch had gone well. Tokara and Peterson didn't seem to have any personal animosity against each other. If anything, they seemed to be good friends. They both were interested in making sure that the election went off without problems, and he was confident that they would make every effort to keep their respective party members in line.

With that bit of business taken care of, the inspector was free to concentrate on his other problem. He'd gotten two names from the hardware store, Frederick Jackson and Ian Bates. A quick check showed that both of them were in the Trust Authority's data base. As he read through the files, there was nothing particularly remarkable in either one of them, certainly nothing that marked either one as the criminal type. Neither had been in any sort of trouble since arriving on Mars, nor did either of them have a criminal record back on Earth. That wasn't surprising, as the screening processes for employment on Mars were pretty thorough.

What did strike McKernan were a number of coincidences. Both men had graduated from the University of Colorado in the same year. Both had attended graduate school in their respective disciplines, and both had received M.S. degrees with decent if not outstanding grades. Both had signed up for standard three year contracts with

Northern & Big Sky Mining, and in fact they had both come out to Mars on the same ship.

There wasn't anything particularly unusual with any of that, McKernan had to admit.   Most of the mining companies recruited from graduating classes, and with the job situation on Earth being what it was, they had their pick of the applicants. Colorado was a good school with a solid program geared toward off-world mining, so it wasn't particularly surprising that several graduates in one year would end up on Mars. In fact, it was something to be expected.

What was out of the ordinary, though, was that both Jackson and Bates hadn't gone back to Earth when their three years were up. Usually, one of two things happened when a contract was up. The most common was that the employee would return to Earth with a fattened bank account and three years of valuable experience under their belts. That was the lure that drew most of the technical types to Mars. The other possibility, though less common, was that the individual would sign up for a second three year contract. There was usually a hefty signing bonus in cases like that; the companies were dealing with a known quantity with experience, and the individual at that point had probably made the decision to become a permanent Martian.

Jackson and Bates had taken neither option. They had chosen to remain on Mars when their contracts had expired, but were not employed by any of the companies or the Trust Authority. While not unheard of, it was unusual, particularly after only a single contract. Less than five percent of the population of Mars fell into the category of the self-employed.

Was it just a coincidence? Even if it wasn't, their actions didn't necessarily have to be construed as sinister. It was quite possible that the two of them had known each other from college. They might well have taken some of the same classes; they might even have been roommates. Even if that wasn't the case, once on Mars they could easily have struck up a friendship on the basis of sharing an alma mater. It would have been a natural thing to occur. And maybe, the two of them had come up with a scheme to get rich and had actually decided to take a chance on it. That was exactly the kind of entrepreneurship that the upcoming election was supposed to foster.

Other than some possibly suspicious purchases, there wasn't anything to tie either of them to the production of the drug Way Back. McKernan continued to examine the files on the two men to find out what they had been doing since their contracts were expired. There wasn't a lot of information available in the data base. They weren't listed as current employees of any of the companies, not even on short term contracts. Neither of them had filed a mining claim during that period. Prospecting and wildcatting were the most common forms of self-employment, but if the two were engaged in those occupations, it didn't look like they weren't doing so on an official basis.

What did that leave? There was salvaging and scavenging, but those were precarious forms of employment. A small number of people were trying to live off the land, but the two didn't fit the profile for that. Most of those people were older, less educated, and there were usually women involved as part of the group.

The two didn't appear to have a residence in Mars City, either, though it was easy enough for someone to find a place to squat in Hut Town without leaving a record. Were the two maintaining some sort of bachelor pad out at the far end of Corridor B? He'd have to have Gaeretts check that possibility out.

The only other official trace the two had left was that they had purchased two Mars buggies, one with a registration number of I-978 and the other with a number of H-145. That supported the notion that the two were engaged in some sort of scheme somewhere in the Out There. Did that scheme involve the manufacture of the memory drug? McKernan knew he didn't yet have enough evidence to act on. For that matter, he didn't have any idea of where Jackson and Martin were.

On a hunch, the inspector ran another query on the computer, this time for any graduates of the University of Colorado who had come to Mars the same year as Jackson and Bates. He wasn't surprised when the search turned up four others.

One, Jacob Wu, could probably be ruled out. He had completed his contract with Anglo-Martian, and had returned to Earth to work on a doctorate in planetary science. A second one, he found to his surprise, he knew. Her name was Julia Hunter, and she was a physician's assistant at the hospital. It seemed unlikely that she would be involved with anything illegal. She had settled in with one of the doctors and, at least according to Beth, was trying to start a family.

The next one that came up was a geologist, Jose Martin. He'd been hired by Rio Plata Mining. McKernan's attention was caught when he saw that Martin had not returned to Earth, nor had he renewed his contract. His current employment status was marked as unknown. Two might just be a coincidence, but three? The inspector was convinced that the three of them were involved in something together.

It was the last name that made the inspector certain that he was on the right track. The name was Jeremy Stanton. His file listed him as having a biology degree, and he had worked for the Trust Authority as a life support system specialist. He, too, had not returned to Earth when his contract expired.

"Gaeretts!" he shouted. The station didn't run to an intercom system, but with the thin walls, that wasn't a problem. A moment later, the sergeant popped his head in the door.

"I take it you've had an epiphany, chief?"

"I think so. Take a look at this." McKernan showed the sergeant the files for the four men.

"I want all the information you can dig up on these four. I want to know where they are right at this moment, and I want to know everything they've been up to for the last year."

"That's not going to be easy if they're somewhere in the Out There."

"I know. But do the best you can. I also want you to send a query to Earth to see if this Jeremy Stanton is any relation of Oliver Stanton. You might make that one through the U.N. Drug Agency."

"I'll get that off right away, chief. Not that I expect them to get back in a hurry. We always seem to be the lowest priority."

"Say it's in reference to the drug Way Back. That might get their attention."

McKernan noticed the curious expression on the sergeant's face.

"Something's got your attention. What is it?"

"It's just that Elena had this notion. She seems to think that the registration on the buggy of her dead man, J-973. She thought it might possibly have originally been I-978 before it had been doctored up with some paint. I just thought I should mention it."

"You thought right. Things are starting to fall into place. Let me know as soon as you find anything out."

McKernan was in no hurry to go home. Beth was working the evening shift at the hospital, so she wouldn't be waiting for him, and he was too keyed up after what he had discovered to want to eat alone. Instead he grabbed dinner from a food cart on the Concourse and headed to Finnegan's for a drink to wash it down.

Finnegan's was the closest thing to an Irish Pub in fifty million kilometers. It was dark, quiet, and the drinks weren't watered down. Finnegan, the owner, had come to Mars under mysterious circumstances and somehow managed to obtain a long term lease on some very desirable real-estate directly across the Concourse from the Mars Club, The Mars Hotel, and the Mars Sheraton. The bar had a real mahogany bar, a battered upright piano slightly out of tune, and an old fashioned dart board which hung just outside the entrance to the men's lavatory.

As usual, Finnegan was minding the bar. He raised an eyebrow when he spotted the inspector, and when the latter nodded, he turned to retrieve a bottle of Scotch from the top shelf of the back bar without asking. He poured a couple of fingers worth of the amber liquid into a glass, paused for a moment and then poured the same into a second glass. He didn't bother with ice or soda. He slid one of the glasses across to McKernan and took the other in his own beefy hand.

"Ready for the election, Erik?"

"As ready as I'll ever be. And you?"

"I'll be glad when it's over. It's been bad for business. All this politicking is keeping people from their drinking," Finnegan said ruefully.

Finnegan's had become the unofficial campaign headquarters for the Red party. The Irishman left no doubts as to where his sympathies lie, but he tried to keep the discourse civil and welcomed both factions to his bar.

"And you, inspector? Will you be glad when it's over?"

"Part of me will, that's for sure. Home rule can't come too soon. It will solve a lot of my problems. I'm just not sure that they'll be my problems anymore."

Finnegan looked the inspector in the eye as if trying to read his mind.

"Oh, I shouldn't worry, Erik. I don't think that either side would want someone else to take your place."

"I wish I was as sure of that as you were."

"Don't be such a pessimist, lad. The companies will support you out of self interest, and Hut Town will back you because you're one of their own. Most of the people out in the provinces trust you more than anyone else. Who does that leave to oppose you but the dead and departed?"

Finnegan was referring to the fact that most of the enemies McKernan had made during his tenure as chief of security had either been killed or sent back to Earth.

"But will people support a security force when they realize they have to pay for it?" McKernan asked, tipping his glass up and emptying it.

"Oh, they'll find a way. They may complain about it a bit, but they'll find a way. Can I pour you another?"

"No. I'd better not. I have this feeling that I'm going to have a busy day tomorrow."

CHAPTER 17

As Elena started to examine the images, she thought about the case. She had a lot of questions as to the how, where, and who, but the one that was really bothering her was the why.

She was pretty sure that the man whose body she had found had killed himself. There had been no signs of foul play, and the evidence pointed to the fact that he had been alone when it had happened. The only logical conclusion was that he had intentionally opened the faceplate of his surface suit. But why had he done so? Had it been a case of suicide? Things like that did happen. Despite all of the psychological screening that took place before someone was allowed on Mars, some people just could not handle the environment. They either developed claustrophobia from living in a confined space or agoraphobia from the wide empty spaces of the Martian surface, or, as happened sometimes, they just couldn't handle the isolation and loneliness. Usually, such people were spotted and sent home or they voluntarily returned to Earth, but not always. The reality was that Mars provided plenty of opportunities for death, particularly in the Out There away from the safe confines of Mars City.

It was certainly possible that the man she had found had intended to kill himself, but for some reason Elena just wasn't comfortable with that answer. There had been no note, and while it was true that suicides don't always leave one, it was common for there to be a last explanation, if only to lay blame on those who remained amongst the living.   Instead, the dead man had been travelling anonymously in a vehicle with a faked registration number. Why?

And why had someone bothered to remove the body? Why try to make it appear as if the death had never happened?   Whoever had removed the body must have known that it had been found. After all, they had gone to some pains to hide the tarp she had laid over the body. And who were they? It occurred to her that there must have been at least two of them, one driving whatever vehicle they had arrived in, and one to drive the dead man's buggy away. But who were they? Had they been enemies of the dead man, or his partners?

Elena thought the latter was more likely. If someone had been after him, the dead man would have been close enough to Junction 3 to radio for help. He hadn't done so. But if it had been his partners who had spirited the body away, why had they done so? They could just have reported it. It was a clear case of suicide and they wouldn't have been blamed. Or they could have done nothing. They knew body had been found. They could have just left it at that and driven away.

But they hadn't. Why? The only answer was because they were trying to hide something. The obvious conclusion was that they wanted to keep whatever they were doing in the Out There a secret. Again, Elena thought the question was why? Had they found something in the area northwest of Junction 3 that they wanted to keep to themselves, a mother load, a big strike? Maybe they had been afraid that one of the mining companies would cheat them out of their find. Or, maybe what they had found infringed on someone else's claim and they were mining it in secret. If that was the case, though, how could they handle the refining and selling the results? They couldn't just show up at Mars City with ingots of semiconductors and sell them. Unless they had found something smaller and easier to smuggle back to Earth like gem stones. Would Martian emeralds or rubies be worth enough to justify the secrecy? Elena had no idea. Jewelry didn't play a part in her life.

There was, of course, another possibility. Despite the extensive efforts of scientists, no signs of Martian life, however microscopic, had ever been discovered. Had the three mystery men stumbled across a Martian fossil? Such a find might prove valuable, if the Trust Authority didn't claim in. Was that the reason behind the secrecy? Or had they found something even more astounding like the ruins of a long lost Martian civilization? A genuine Martian artifact would be literally priceless. Elena knew that the idea was ridiculous, but every so often rumors would trickle out of the Out There of someone finding—something. Usually, the rumors could be traced back to someone playing a joke or telling a tall tale over drinks, but that didn't stop the rumors from happening. Maybe, Elena thought, Mars, like Earth, needed its legends and ghost stories. But were the stories all just stories?

Elena realized that this was all wild speculation. She also realized that her soup was getting cold. The only way to find an answer to the why was to figure out what the dead man and his partners had been doing in the Out There, and right now she could only hope to find some trace in the images that Gaeretts had sent her.

She spent the next hour going through the images. She hadn't found much. There were no obvious surface operations that weren't accounted for. She had found one image that showed lots of activity and a big pile of mine tailings, but when she checked the coordinates she found that they matched those of one of Anglo-Martian's camps. Did she need to widen her search area? Or did she need to look for subtler traces?

She had the approximate location of where Gus had said he'd spotted a buggy whose registration might have matched the dead man's. She pulled up the highest resolution image that she had at those coordinates. When she blew it up to examine it in detail, she could see tracks in the dust. They weren't continuous, just where the dust was thick enough to take tire impressions, but there were the tracks of multiple vehicles, multiple vehicles or the same vehicle making multiple trips.

The tracks were all aligned in a roughly north-south direction. She pulled up a terrain map. Heading south, there was a fairly easy path that would meet up with the road about eighty kilometers to the west of Junction 3. It wasn't exactly a road, but someone who was familiar with the route could make pretty good time over the route.

It wasn't the connection to the road that was of interest, though, it was the direction the tracks were headed. Elena followed the tracks to the north edge of the image, then, pulled up an image directly to the north of the one she had been examining. It took her a moment to align the features to orient the two, but when she had, she was able to spot a continuation of the tracks. She followed the tracks across the image and then on to the next one.

The farther north she looked the rougher the terrain was getting. The region had obviously been the site of some volcanism in the ancient past of Mars. In many places the surface was hard lava blown clear of dust, so that it didn't take tire impressions well. Elena found her eyes straining to pick out the tire marks in the few depressions where dust had collected.

The tracks led roughly north for almost two hundred kilometers from the road before they seemed to end. Elena couldn't spot any continuation of the tracks, but she wasn't sure whether because they didn't extend any farther, or because the terrain just didn't retain any signs of vehicles passing.

She spent nearly fifteen minutes examining images trying to pick up the trail before giving up the effort. If the tracks went farther, she was convinced that she wasn't going to find them in the images. Instead, she returned to the image with the last tracks she had found and began to pour over it looking for traces of human activity.

If the partners had been operating in that area, she would have expected to be able to spot some indication. There should at least have been a hut or a solar cell array or a parked vehicle even if most of their workings were underground, but if there was, it wasn't showing in the image. About all she could spot was a place right at the end of the trail where the vehicle tracks went back and forth in different directions as if buggies had been driven over the same area repeatedly.

If that was the site of their works, where were all the signs of their activities, Elena thought? Any sort of operation would need at least a power source, even if everything else was underground. That usually meant a fairly large collection of solar cells, but nothing like that was visible in the images. Did that mean they were using a nuclear reactor? Elena thought it unlikely. Those were expensive, closely controlled, and used only for the largest and most permanent installations.

In frustration, Elena looked for other images of the same area. She found one that was of lower resolution, but which had been taken at a different time of day. She knew enough about imagery to know that objects could sometimes be revealed not by their direct image, but by their shadows. The image she pulled up had been taken late in the day when the sun was close to the horizon. Shadows traced long dark lines across the red dust of the surface.

She wasn't an expert at that sort of thing, so it took her a long time to orient herself and identify which shadows were being cast by which physical features. She stared at the image until her eyes burned, trying to pick out something that might not be there. Finally she thought she saw something. She wasn't quite sure why she thought so, but it didn't seem to be a natural feature. It struck her as being manmade, though she couldn't have told anyone what she thought it was.

She checked the time. It was 2300. She had stayed up way too long, especially as she wanted to make an early start of it in the morning. She wanted to get an early start because she finally thought she knew where she should be looking.

CHAPTER 18

When McKernan got to the station the next morning, he could tell from the expression on his sergeant's face, that he had some hot information for him. He stalled him for the moment by asking, "Have you heard anything from Elena?"

"Yeah. She drove her usual patrol out to Junction 4 yesterday. As far as I know, nothing new has turned up about her missing corpse. She did ask for a bunch of imagery of the area to the northwest of Junction 3. I gathered up what I could find and sent it out to Junction 4 so it would be waiting for her. There was quite a lot of it. So far I haven't heard back from her. As far as I know she was planning on driving back home today."

"Let me know when she check's in."

"Sure thing, chief," Gaeretts responded laconically.

"Anything else I should know about?"

"We got a response to that enquiry you had me send to Earth. You must have been right about Way Back being the magic word. At least it got someone's attention Earthside."

"And?" McKernan asked impatiently.

"It turns out that this Oliver Stanton has a nephew named Jeremy Stanton. The agency didn't have much information on him because he's never been associated with the drug business, but the age matches the Jeremy Stanton on Mars. It might just be a coincidence—"

"But for the moment we'll treat it as if it isn't," McKernan clarified. "Any word on his location? Or that of his three friends?"

"Nothing definite. But I did show their photos to the constables who were working shifts last night to see if they recognized any of them."

"And?"

"Ferris thought he recognized one of them. Bates. It seems that he has a hut out towards the end of B Corridor. Apparently he doesn't live there full time, but he uses it when he's in Mars City. Ferris had the impression that he might be sharing it with several others, but he's never seen them so he couldn't say if one of them was Stanton or any of the others you're interested in."

"How'd Bates come by the hut?"

"Usual situation. The guy that lived there before was going back to Earth. They worked out some sort of deal, and Bates took possession when he left. You know how it is?"

McKernan did know. He'd acquired his own home in essentially the same manner. Theoretically, the Trust Authority held title to all of Hut Town, or at least the ground that it was built on. The huts themselves belonged to whoever had put them up, which usually meant one of the companies. But the huts had mostly been abandoned when the permanent part of Mars City had been built, and few objections had been raised when squatters had started to move in. As the saying went, possession was nine tenths of the law, but there was no law on Mars, so no one in Hut Town had a clear title no matter how long they had occupied their hut. Sorting out the land claims was going to be one of the major tasks facing the eventual government if home rule became a reality.

"So, for all we know, this hut might be nothing more than a shared bachelor pad for wildcatters to crash in when they're in town?"

"That's pretty much the size of it," Gaeretts agreed.

"What shift was Ferris working?"

"He had the early evening shift."

"He's had time to get some sleep then. Give him a call and tell him I want to see him as soon as possible. I think we may want to pay this hut a visit, and I'd like to know what the lay of the land is before we do so."

Ferris showed up about an hour later, sleepy but eager.

"Gaeretts said you wanted to see me, sir?"

McKernan reflected that the constable was no longer a fresh faced kid straight from Earth. He was on his second contract, and gave all the signs of becoming a permanent Martian. He still looked younger than his years, but there was a hardness behind his baby face that was hard to miss. Five years of settling bar fights and dealing with drunks would do that to a man. Even here in the security station his eyes constantly darted around the room as if on guard.

"Yeah, he said that you recognized one of the men I'm interested in."

"Yes, sir. He's got a place out at the end of Hut Town."

"I want to hear all about that place."

McKernan got up from his desk and told Ferris to follow him to the conference room. Along the way he motioned for Gaeretts to join them. Once they had gotten seated, the inspector flashed the images of Bates, Martin, Stanton, and Jackson on the wall display.

"These are the four men I'm interested in. Do you recognize any of them?"

"The only one I'm sure about is the one on the end. His name is Bates. Or at least that's the one he's been using."

"That's his name, alright. Ian Bates. He was working as a chemical engineer until his contract was up. What I'd like to know is what he's been up to the last year."

"I'm not sure if I can tell you anything, sir. Like I said, he's got a hut out at the end of Corridor B, but I don't think he's there most of the time. He seems to spend a lot of time somewhere in the Out There, but I'm not sure where."

"What about the others? "

"Maybe. Maybe not. They're all kind of average looking, aren't they? White, late twenties, middle height and build. No distinguishing features or visible tattoos. They look like about half the population of Mars. I can't remember ever having a run in with any of them. I certainly don't remember having seen them around recently."

McKernan knew that he could believe his constable. Ferris mostly patrolled the far end of Hut Town, the part with all the bars and bordellos. That was where the trouble occurred. He'd know who he needed to watch out for. As far as everybody else, if they didn't cause trouble, they weren't his concern.

"OK. What about this Bates? Have you ever had trouble with him?"

"No. Not really, sir. It's just that I remember him. Like I said, he's got this hut. I've noticed people entering or leaving every once in a while. Not the same people. Different ones every time. I thought he might be running a floating poker game or something like that, or maybe an unregistered whore house, but when I asked around, no one admitted to knowing anything about it. There were never any complaints, so I just kind of filed the information away just in case. You know how it is, sir?"

"Yeah, I know how it is," McKernan replied. He'd done his share of patrols at the end of Hut Town when he'd first come to Mars. "What can you tell me about this hut?"

"Nothing much. I've never seen the inside. As far as I know, it's just an ordinary residential hut. The guy that lived there before certainly wasn't into anything dodgy. He just wanted a little privacy and space. Bates took it over from him when the original occupant went back to Earth."

McKernan brought up a map of Hut Town on the display. "Which one is it?"

Ferris fiddled with the computer for a moment, blowing up a section of the end of Corridor B. There was a string of huts flanking the corridor, all the same, about fifteen meters long and eight meters wide. He used the cursor to highlight a hut in the middle of the string.

"That's the one, sir."

McKernan looked more closely at the map. Ferris was right, it was just a standard residential hut. It wasn't much different than his own, except that now he had two huts that were adjacent to each other with an airlock between joining them. None of the huts on the map had been combined.

"Do you know if it has a back door?" McKernan asked. He was referring to an airlock that gave access out onto the surface. Some huts had them, some didn't.

"I think so. Most of the huts along there do," Ferris answered.

"Do you happen to know if Bates is home at the moment?"

"I haven't seen him lately," Ferris said. "Of course I haven't been looking for him."

"I guess we'll have to play it as if he's home, then," McKernan announced.

"I take it you want to get a look at the inside of that hut?" Gaerretts asked.

"That's the idea," McKernan confirmed.

"Sir, do you mind my asking what this is about?" Ferris queried.

"It's possible that Bates and the other three men whose pictures I showed you have something to do with the manufacture and distribution of a drug that has been causing people to forget they're on Mars. I want to find out for sure."

"You mean Memory Dust?" Ferris asked.

"That's one of its names. Way Back and Playback are others. What do you know about it, Ferris?" McKernan asked sharply.

"Just that there's been word going around in the corridors about it. Mostly, it's been rumors I've picked up. I've never actually talked to anyone who admitted to using it, but people seem to know it's out there."

"Well, we know some people have been using it. Just ask Dr. Greenwood."

"What exactly are you planning, chief?" Gaeretts asked.

"I want to stage a raid on this hut, just the three of us. Gaeretts and I will come in off the corridor. Ferris, you'll suit up and make sure that no one bolts out the back airlock. You'd better take a riot gun."

"Do you think that will be needed, sir?" Ferris asked, nervous and excited at the same time.

A shotgun on Mars was a pretty serious weapon, especially on the surface where a single pellet could breech the surface suit or crack the helmet of anyone who got in the way of the blast.

"I don't want to take any chances. What I want to make sure of is that no one gets away and no one has a chance to destroy evidence."

"Yes, sir."

"What are we going to be packing?" Gaeretts asked. "People are going to get nervous if they see us toting riot guns through the Concourse."

"Pistols should be good enough. I doubt if anyone will get past us in the airlock. But I want you to grab the forensic kit. We'll want to look for fingerprints and make images of whatever we find. We'll probably need to collect evidence, as well. Do you both understand what we're doing?"

Both Ferris and Gaeretts nodded.

"Good. It's almost 1000 now. Let's plan on going in at 1100. That will give Ferris time to get suited up and get out to the end of Corridor B. Gaeretts and I will wait until you get in position and then come in through the airlock off the corridor. Ferris, you call us when you're ready."

CHAPTER 19

Elena had risen early so that she could get started on her way back to Junction 3 as soon as it was light enough to drive. There wasn't really much of a drawback to getting up that early, breakfast in the dining room at Junction 4 ran to powdered eggs and freeze dried fried potatoes; nothing near as good as what Jenny would be serving at the Junction 3 hotel. As usual, Lewis was starved for company and wanted to gossip, but she begged off, even when he offered her a second cup of coffee.

She had an ulterior motive for starting so early. The run back home normally took about ten hours without stops, which would put her into Junction 3 around 1600. If she pushed things a little, she could make an excursion a few hours north off the road and still be at Junction 3 before Miguel's bedtime. Even allowing for the fact that she would be travelling off road once she headed north, she thought should be able to go about seventy or eighty kilometers north before she needed to turn back.

From looking over the imagery the previous night, she had a pretty good idea of the most likely route someone would drive from the road to meet up with the tracks of the buggy Gus had spotted. It had mostly been a matter of seeking out the flattest terrain on a route that skirted major obstacles. She had plotted it out last night and transferred the route map into the buggy's computer.

An hour out of Junction 4, she was pushing the buggy to nearly seventy kilometers an hour, about as fast as the drive motors could handle. Usually, she drove at a more sedate fifty, but on the road there wasn't really much danger in driving faster. It's not as if there was traffic to worry about, and she hadn't seen any fresh obstacles driving the other way. The only vehicle she passed was a freight hauler headed out from Mars City. She hadn't known the driver, and other than a perfunctory greeting, neither of them had paused to exchange gossip.

Just after 1100 she made a brief stop for lunch, mostly to have an opportunity to stretch her cramped muscles and use what had charitably been termed a toilet by the buggy's designers. Lunch consisted of a couple of ration bars and water mixed with some "grape" flavor powder. She preferred the orange or even the cherry, but she was running low on both and still had plenty of the grape. Having fresh fruit was one of the things about Earth that she missed the most. Many vegetables were easy enough to grow on Mars, but anything that came on a tree was scarce. They required too much time to grow and took up too much space and water. Jenny's husband had been experimenting with a few trees, but it would be years before his efforts bore fruit. Elena groaned at her own pun.

She made a second stop at the point where she planned to turn off the road. She had made better time than she had thought and it was just after 1200. After she used the toilet again, she took the opportunity to put on her surface suit. She preferred to drive without one because they were uncomfortable for long periods of time, but she didn't know when she'd come across something that she might want to examine close up. Being in the suit already would cut her time for an EVA, and she knew she was cutting things close as it was. She dumped the suit's helmet on the seat next to her where it would be handy.

Off the road she drove more slowly, about thirty five. Early on, the going was actually pretty good, and this close to the road there were plenty of tracks from other vehicles to follow. The route she had picked out led through a pass some thirty kilometers north of the road that was a natural funnel for anyone heading north. The pass was a flat break about a kilometer wide in a low ridge that ran more or less due east-west.

After emerging on the far side of the pass, the tracks that she had been following spread out in either direction. That was what she had expected. The pass served as a bottleneck, and once through, the earlier vehicles had turned off towards whatever their final destination had been. There were still a number of tracks, though, that lead in the direction she was headed. She had no idea if they had been made by the people she was interested in or someone else.

Elena admitted to herself that she had no idea what it was she expected to find. The site she had identified in the imagery had been nearly three hundred kilometers north of the road. She wouldn't be able to go much more than a hundred before she would need to turn back if she still wanted to make it to Junction 3 that evening. Still, she had felt the need to do something, and it was possible that she'd find some trace of the dead man or his partners along the way.

For a moment, she thought about continuing on north. The buggy held more than enough supplies to allow such a trip. They had been designed for long distance exploration, and Mike made sure that hers was always in tip top shape and fully stocked. It was a tempting idea, but she decided not to. Her closest backup was Kaminski and he was probably twelve hundred kilometers off to the west. She'd learned to play it cautiously, and with Mike and Miguel she had too much to lose. She'd drive north a hundred kilometers and then turn back in time to tuck Miguel into bed.

The terrain north of the pass was rougher, but she still had tracks to follow, though that was about all she saw. Mars can be a monotonous place, and the parts she was driving through had a tendency to look the same. If she hadn't had the navigation signals from the positioning satellites, she could easily have gotten herself lost.

It was a little after 1500 when she reached the coordinates where Gus had spotted the buggy. She slowed down, looking for landmarks that she might recognize from the satellite images. After hunting around for a few minutes, she found what she thought were the tracks Gus had left. She positioned her buggy alongside them and got out a pair of binoculars.

She scanned the landscape in the direction that Gus said he had been looking, but there really wasn't much to see, just dust and rocks. The shadows were starting to lengthen, which only reminded her that it was close to the time when she would have to turn back.

She started driving slowly in the direction Gus had indicated. Sure enough, after driving a kilometer she picked up the track of a buggy headed north. She was pretty sure it was the mystery buggy the old surveyor had spotted, the one with the partial ID J-9. She started to follow the tracks, driving parallel with them but twenty meters to the side so as not to confuse the trail.

The dust was thinner ahead of her, leaving bare rock where the wind had uncovered it. This made the trail harder to follow, requiring all her concentration to keep from losing it. Elena was thinking that it was about time to give up. She'd found the trail, but the she knew the other end was a six or seven hour drive north. She didn't have that time.

Suddenly there was a loud pop and the low pressure alarm started to sound. Elena didn't bother to look for the cause. Her only thought was to get her helmet secured. The buggy was losing pressure fast.

She grabbed the helmet from the seat next to her, trying to keep from panicking. She knew that she had time to get it on if she worked methodically. For an instant she thought the neck ring had jammed, but then the helmet rotated into place. She went through the suit check, turning on life support and making sure that suit integrity was holding. It was.

Only when she was sure she could survive on suit air did she try to determine what had happened. It didn't take long for her to find the cause. There was a small, circular hole in the Plexiglas of the right forward viewing bubble. It was about the diameter of a thumb. The Plexiglas had been starred around the hold but it hadn't cracked. If she could plug the hole, pressure could be restored.

She grabbed the first thing she could find, a plastic pouch that had held one of the ration bars she had had for lunch. She slapped it over the hole. The pressure of the evacuating air held it in place. She could see a dimple in the bag forming as it was sucked into the hole, but for the moment the plastic held. That gave her time to act.

The buggy had an emergency depressurization kit, essentially a box of bandages for surface suits or any other pressurized device. The kit was held in a clip next to the airlock hatch. Elena got up, went to the hatch, and popped the kit open. She fumbled through the contents until she found a patch of about the right size.

She went back up to the front of the buggy. The patch was held in a wrapper that was designed to be easy to open while wearing a surface suit. Still, it took her two tries to get it open. The patch itself was a small disk about five centimeters in diameter. One side was covered with a contact adhesive. The sides were color coded so you couldn't make a mistake. She pulled the ration bar pouch off the hole and slapped the patch on over the hole, pressing it tightly to make sure that the adhesive took.

The pressure alarm stopped sounding. The patch was holding and the buggy's life support system was restoring pressure. Elena realized that she had been breathing rapidly, almost to the point of overloading her suit. She made a conscious effort to slow her breathing and pulse rate, reassuring herself that things were going to be alright. She took a few measured breathes. Then she went back to the patch kit, grabbed another, larger patch and slapped it over the first one.

Finally able to breathe easily, Elena tried to think what had caused the breach. Her first thought was that a rock had been kicked up by her buggy, but she rejected that idea right away. A rock wouldn't have been travelling fast enough to punch a hole in the viewport, and besides the buggy would have thrown it backwards, not up in front of itself. Her next thought was that she had been hit by a meteorite. That wasn't as farfetched as it sounded. A small meteorite could easily have been travelling fast enough to do the damage, and the atmosphere of Mars didn't provide much in the way of protection. It would have been a fluke occurrence, but flukes did happen.

The only problem with that, was that judging from the part of the viewport that had been hit, the meteorite would have to have been travelling almost horizontally.

Whatever it had been, Elena thought that she might be able to find it or at least a fragment of it. She got up, turned on the interior illumination of the buggy and began an examination of the cabin.

She found the fragment embedded in the cover of one of the aft storage compartments. The cover was hard plastic, but the meteor had penetrated nearly a centimeter deep. She used a multi-tool from the belt of her surface suit to pry the fragment out. That was when Elena realized it hadn't been a meteorite. She'd had enough experience with firearms to recognize a spent bullet when she saw one. Following a line from the hole in the storage cover to the front bubble she saw that the bullet had missed her head by a matter of centimeters.

Rushing to the front, she grabbed the binoculars and scanned the landscape in front of her. She couldn't see anything, but the terrain provided plenty of places for a sniper to hide. She was pretty sure that whoever had shot her had been using a rifle. Anyone close enough to have used a pistol would have been close enough to be seen.

Elena realized that she was a sitting duck. There was an assault rifle and a riot gun in a locked compartment in the back of the buggy, but even if she could see the sniper, there was no way that she could fire either weapon from inside the buggy. Besides, the buggy was standing out in the open and the sniper was obviously behind cover. Even if she did exit the buggy, she'd still be an easy target.

Elena did the only thing that she could; she turned the buggy around and headed back the way she had come driving as fast as she could. Whatever sort of weapon the sniper was using, he'd demonstrated that the buggy wouldn't provide her much protection.

It was twenty minutes of driving before Elena felt she was safe enough to pop the faceplate of her suit. In that time she'd put ten or more kilometers between her and the sniper. She stopped the buggy and did an inspection of the patch. It seemed to be holding.

Elena knew she was too far from the road for her phone to work, but the buggy had a satellite radio. She tried to contact one of the relay satellites, but none of them were in range. A quick check of the computer showed that it would be another half hour before one was overhead. There was nothing for her to do but keep driving south.

It was only due to the sun's being low on the horizon that allowed her to spot the shadow extending across the sand. Someone had stuck a metal rod into the surface to make an improvised marker.

CHAPTER 20

The three of them looked innocent enough as they crossed the Concourse. The fact that Ferris was wearing a surface suit and carrying a helmet, drew a few curious stares, but no more. Despite living in a safely enclosed environment, the residents of Mars City were well aware that they were surrounded by a hostile planet that could easily kill an unprepared man in a dozen different ways. They would have been more attentive if they had noticed that he was carrying a riot gun, but Ferris had had the sense to leave that in its case, just another piece of anonymous apparatus.

A few of the people who observed them crossing the Concourse may have realized that something was up. You didn't often see three members of the security force together, especially when one of them was suited up to go outside. There just weren't enough constables for that to be a common occurrence. If anyone did realize what was happening, none of them bothered to ask questions. Most people on Mars would recognize McKernan, and most of them were content to let him go about his business. For good or ill, the chief inspector had a reputation.

Corridor B started on the far side of the Concourse. For the first hundred meters, it looked no different than any other part of Mars City, a wide hallway with walls of fused silicon blocks broken at intervals by air-tight doors. Behind the doors were the offices of various companies and departments of the Trust Authority, usually, but not always marked by discrete signage. At the hundred meter point, the hallway terminated in an airlock. The airlock was always kept closed except when people were going through it. It marked the boundary between Mars City proper and Hut Town.

Gaeretts pushed the button that opened the door and started the airlock cycle. The three policeman stepped through the lock door when it opened, closing it behind them. Because both sides of the airlock were kept at roughly the same pressure, there was little delay before the hatch on the far side of the lock chamber opened.

The corridor they entered was different in nature than the one they had left. This one had been formed by inflating a tube of what was essentially aluminum foil, spraying on a coating of insulating foam, and then fitting it out with flooring, lighting, and other fixtures. Because this length of corridor was the closest to Mars City and had been the last to be completed, the workmen had taken more pains with the fit and finish, but it was still part of the old part of Mars, the pneumatic architecture that had been meant to be temporary but which continued to exist decades later because it still served a purpose.

This first section of Corridor B was respectably commercial. The airlocks that broke the sides gave way to various enterprises that provided goods, services, and support to the community. The floor might still be made of panels that could be easily removed to allow access to the piping and cabling that ran underneath, but they were swept daily to remove any dust that might have been carried in from outside. The corridor temperature was kept at a cool but comfortable 18 degrees Celsius.

There were plans in progress to make the first sections of the corridors more permanent, replacing the tube with silicon bricks and covering the corridor with a half meter of soil for radiation shielding. Work had already started on Corridor C, but questions of who should pay for the work was retarding progress. Until the ownership of the huts linked to the corridor was settled, no one was willing to make the commitment.

The three men reached the end of the first section of corridor to face another airlock. They quickly cycled through into the next segment. Here the floor sloped up slightly. After the next airlock, the corridor tubing had been laid above ground because it had been cheaper and quicker. The air was dryer and cooler, though still not unpleasant. The floor had still been swept recently.

They passed through several more airlocks and the neighborhood turned residential, airlocks every ten meters or so providing access to huts that had been adapted to private homes. This close to Mars City, Hut Town was still respectable. In fact, the McKernan's own hut was along this section of the corridor.

The transition was gradual. After they had passed through the section where Mckernan lived, there was a gradual relaxing of standards. It was nothing major, nothing that would compromise life support, but it was noticeable in the little things. The temperature dropped. A few of the light fixtures weren't working. The dust from outside tended to collect in corners and not be swept up.

The far ends of the corridors, especially the three middle ones, B, C, and D, were the least desirable parts of Hut Town, essentially a red light district. The huts in the last few segments had either been abandoned or turned into bars, brothels or bordellos whose existence was tolerated if not encouraged.

The hut Bates had taken up as his residence was in the section just before the most active part of the far end. The three paused in the airlock between sections to make final plans.

"Do you want me to go out the airlock at the end of the corridor, sir?" Ferris asked as he prepared to put his helmet on.

"It's probably quicker to use the access hatch in the cross tunnel," Gaeretts pointed out. McKernan just nodded.

Ferris twisted on his helmet and ran through a suit check with the sergeant double checking everything. The constable might never be more than a few dozen meters away, but once outside, that wouldn't matter. Satisfied that his suit integrity was holding, he removed the riot gun from its case. There was a side hatch leading to a tunnel connecting to Corridor A. Ferris opened it and went through.

McKernan and Gaeretts waited in the airlock. It wasn't a long wait. In less than five minutes the call came that Ferris was in position.

"Ready?" McKernan asked. He had drawn a small automatic pistol and was holding it close to his leg.

Gaeretts nodded, his own pistol out. He punched the button to open the airlock door.

Bates's hut was behind the fourth airlock on the left. They quickly moved to flank the hatch. Gaeretts hit the comm button and shouted, "Security. Open up." There was no mention of a search warrant. One wasn't needed. Mars, at least currently, didn't have laws protecting privacy.

There was no response. The hatch didn't have a locking mechanism, but a padlock and hasp had been installed. They'd expected that. Gaeretts had a bolt cutter with him that made short work of the lock. A quick check showed the inside of the lock held air. The sergeant opened the hatch. With two of them, it was a tight fit. The telltale on the inner hatch revealed that the hut was pressurized as well. The hatch operated manually. McKernan undogged it and then kicked it open.

The hut was in darkness, the only illumination being provided by a viewport at the far end. McKernan peered around the flange of the hatch, trying to penetrate the gloom in the corners. As far as he could tell, the hut was unoccupied.

He stepped over the lip of the hatch opening and moved to the side so that he wouldn't be silhouetted against the airlock light. It took him a moment to find the switch for the lights. When he did, a couple of panels lit up. The place was empty.

"Kind of anticlimactic, isn't it?" Gaerett commented.

"That's fine by me," the inspector responded before speaking into his radio, "Anyone come out, Ferris?"

"Nothing, sir. No recent foot prints, either. It doesn't look like the lock has been used in a few weeks."

"You might as well come in, then. See if you can use the backdoor airlock."

A few moments later they could hear the sounds of the airlock cycling. While they waited for the constable, they took a quick look around.

The hut was cold. Not freezing, but chilly, as if it hadn't been used in a while. The air had a dry, desiccated scent to it layered on top of the smell of bad cooking and body odor. That didn't make for a pleasant combination.

The furnishings were Spartan at best. Four mattresses had been laid on the floor, two of them holding a tangle of blankets and bedding. The cooking facilities consisted of a pressure pot and a microwave. The contents of the refrigerator amounted to a few jugs of water, a couple of beer bottles, and an opened can of condensed milk. When McKernan smelled it, he could tell it was spoiled. The food supplies amounted to a couple of dozen ration packs and some dried beans.

"Not particularly neat, were they?" Gaeretts said. Martians, like sailors, tended to be orderly in their domestic arrangements; space was at a premium, and knowing where everything was might save your life.

"I don't think Bates, or anyone else, was living here on a permanent basis," McKernan responded. As he did so, Ferris came out of the rear airlock. He gave the place a quick once over, set his shotgun against the wall and then popped his helmet.

"I take it we missed them, sir?"

"Looks like. We'll need to take pictures and prints, though," McKernan said. "Then we need to give the place a thorough search."

"Is it alright if I get out of this suit first, sir?"

"Go ahead. I don't think you'll be needing it again."

Gaeretts helped the constable out of his suit. Fortunately the latter had brought along a coverall and some shoes in the carrying bag he had for his surface suit so that he was able to look respectable and comfortable after a few minutes. Both the inspector and the sergeant had managed to look elsewhere during the transition.

Once he had changed, Ferris started the process of imaging the inside of the hut. He knew that his superiors intended to leave the technical business to him. Besides, he rather enjoyed the work. It was more interesting than dealing with drunks.

"If you don't need me, chief, maybe I should be getting back," Gaeretts said. "Someone should be there to mind the store."

McKernan looked up, distracted for a moment, then, he agreed. "Sure, go ahead. It doesn't look like you'll be needed."

McKernan waited while Ferris finished up with the camera work. While he waited, he did a walk through from the front of the hut to the back. The basic layouts of the huts were pretty similar. They had been mass produced on Earth to be set up as temporary quarters on Mars. There was an airlock in the front which was flanked by the life support module on one side and a small bathroom area on the other. The rest of the hut was an open area about twelve meters long and eight meters wide. The idea had been that it could be fitted out with temporary partitions as needed, but it looked as though no one had ever bothered to do so with this one. Either that, or someone had scavenged the partitions and anything else useful before Bates had moved in.

The mattresses had been lined up along either wall, two on a side. Some boxes had been set up as seating and a makeshift table. There were a couple of other containers and what looked like a tool chest. A quick look inside revealed some wrenches, a couple of screw drivers, pliers, and some electrical tape and wire nuts. Nothing unusual there. The rest of the place just looked unsettled.

"Notice anything, Ferris?" he asked finally.

"What's that, sir?" the constable replied after a quick glance around.

"No plants." Almost every Martian who had the space for it grew plants. They provided food, replenished the air, and just made things seem more homey. The back third of the inspector's own hut was given over to a container garden. There weren't any plants growing in this hut, nor signs that there ever had been. How did that fit in with his theory about Way Back?

"That *is* odd," Ferris agreed. "Maybe they knew that no one would be around to take care of them. Plants require a lot of care, sir."

"I think you're right about that, constable. From what I can see whoever was using this place was only using it for a day or two at a time. If they had been spending more time here they'd have fixed it up. The question is what were they doing the rest of the time?"

"I'm done with the pictures, sir. Where do you want me to check for prints?"

"Might as well do the airlock and life support controls and the cooking gear. Don't waste too much time on it. Then we're going to tear this place apart. I don't care if it takes the rest of the day. I think there's something hidden here and I want to find it."

CHAPTER 21

Constable Ortiz stopped the buggy close to the marker. It would be dark soon, and she still had a long drive ahead of her if she was going to get home that night. Chances were that the marker was nothing important, nothing more than a reference point left by some prospector or surveyor months or years earlier to help find something that was of no interest to her or anyone else. But why was it here at this particular location, a location on the trail used by the mysterious group to the North?

Elena hadn't noticed it on the drive up from the road, but at that time of day it would have been easy to miss. Even now, near dusk, she might easily have missed it if she had been driving twenty or thirty meters to the east or west. The rod was just a few centimeters in diameter and only a meter or so of its length protruded above the surface.

The question was, what was she going to do about it? She already had her surface suit on and was stopped. She might as well go and check it out. It would only take a few minutes.

As she cycled through the airlock, she noted the levels in the air supply reserves. The buggy had lost some oxygen and nitrogen through the leak before she had managed to patch it, but there were still plenty of both left. Mike never let her leave for patrol without making sure everything was topped up. Sometimes she objected to his fussing over her. Now she thought that she'd have to stop that.

As she stepped out onto the surface she looked nervously around her. Though she had driven a dozen kilometers from where she had been shot at, she still felt like a sitting duck. Staring at the horizon searching for a non-existent sniper wasn't going to get her anywhere, though.

There was nothing special about the metal pole. It looked to be steel with corrugations marking its surface every centimeter or so. It was probably a piece of reinforcing rod used in construction, Elena thought to herself. She grabbed the rod with one of her suit's gloves and gave it a wiggle. There wasn't much movement. It had been lodged pretty firmly into the surface. Giving it a close examination, it appeared that the top of the rod had been hit with repeated blows from a hammer, probably while it was being driven into the dust.

Elena stepped back a few steps to get perspective. The dust on the surface to one side of the stake looked as if it had been disturbed. There was a faint depression and the color seemed different than the surrounding area as if the surface dust had been mixed with some from deeper down. It looked as if something had been buried and the location marked by the rod.

She noted the time. The sun would be below the horizon in a half an hour. Then it would be dark. With no air, Mars didn't have extended periods of twilight. With her recent experience in mind she knew that if she was going to do something she had to do it quickly.

She walked back to get a shovel from the buggy's tool bin and started digging. She hoped that whoever had dug the hole hadn't dug it deep. The sand in the hole was loose, looser than the surroundings. It took the constable only a few minutes before the shovel hit something. Brushing away the dust to see what it was, she saw what looked like the fabric of a surface suit. Elena had found a body.

Able to figure out the orientation of the body, she cleared the dust away from the helmet. The faceplate had been closed and it was hard to see using the only the lights from the helmet of her surface suit, but Elena was pretty sure it was the same man whose body she had found on the road.

She sighed. It was going to take a while to dig the body up, but she wasn't going to leave it. Not this time. She'd already made that mistake once. Determined, she set to work. She wasn't being particularly careful about her digging. She just wanted to clear enough of the sand away so that she could pull the corpse from the ground.

It was full dark by the time she had finished uncovering the grave, and she was operating using the headlights from the buggy for illumination. She bent down to try and lift the body out of the hole she had dug, but it wouldn't pull free. For a moment she sank down in frustration, but she wasn't going to admit defeat. She could spend a few more minutes of digging or she could try something else.

The buggy had a winch mounted on the front. It could be operated from the outside. She spooled out a few meters of cable and managed to snake it under the body to form a loop around the torso snugged against the armpits. She wasn't sure that McKernan would approve of what she was doing to evidence, but she didn't care. She wasn't going to leave the body behind. Not this time.

She used the winch to draw the cable taught and then wound up the cable. The body moved a few centimeters. Using the shovel to leverage up the body, she pulled in a few more centimeters of cable. At this point, she didn't want to tear the body in half. A little more work with the shovel and the top part of the body was free of the hole. From that point, it was easy.

Unhooking the cable, she wound the winch all the way in. For her size, Elena was a strong woman, but she was glad that this was Mars where the gravity was a third of what it was on Earth. The corpse was an awkward thing to handle. It was frozen stiff, wouldn't bend and the arms projected out at odd angles. It was fortunate that she didn't have to try getting the body through the airlock. The buggy had baskets on either side where excess gear and supplies could be stowed. After a couple of tries she managed to tip the corpse into one of these and lash it down with some bungy cords. If anyone had been watching her she suspected that her efforts would have been quite comical. At least, she thought, she wouldn't have to drive home with the body inside keeping her company.

She stowed the rest of her gear and started driving back towards the road.

In the darkness, she could only drive at half the speed she had used on the way up. She didn't bother to try to catch one of the communications satellites. Checking in could wait until she was on the road and driving home. It was nearly 2100 when she finally drove through the pass and was within range of one of the cell towers along the road.

The first call she made was to Mike. Elena knew it wasn't protocol, but she didn't care. Mike had been expecting her home and would be worried sick. And, after all, there wasn't much that either Gaeretts or Inspector McKernan could do about her discoveries that a few minutes delay would matter. They were fifteen hundred kilometers away in Mars City.

"Elena, where are you?" Mike answered frantically. "I've been trying to raise you for the last three hours."

"I had a little problem with the buggy," she answered. No point in explaining the details until her husband could see that she was safe and sound.

"What kind of problem? Why didn't you call? I could have come out and gotten you!"

"The buggy had a pressurization loss." That happens when you're shot at, Elena thought to herself. "I'm fine. I was wearing my surface suit at the time. All I had to do was put on my helmet and slap a patch on the hole. It was over in a matter of minutes. I didn't call you Mike because I didn't want you to worry. Besides I wasn't in communications range."

"What do you mean you weren't in range. There are relay towers all along the road."

"I wasn't on the road, Mike. I was looking into something. I found it, too, or at least part of it."

"What are you talking about?" Mike asked. The frantic tone in his voice was turning to exasperation.

"I'll tell you all about it when I get home, Mike."

"Where are you now?"

"I'm on the road, about seventy-five kilometers out. I should be home in less than an hour and a half. Look, I've got to check in with Gaeretts. Love you, Mike. Tell Miguel goodnight for me if he's still up. Bye."

She terminated the call and made another one to headquarters before Mike had a chance to call her back.

Gaeretts answered. He didn't mention it, but she could hear the concern in his voice. "Kind of late to be checking in, isn't it constable?"

"I've been kind of busy, sarge. Investigating. I've got a couple of things to report."

"Go ahead, Ortiz. Make my night."

"Well the first thing is I've been right. There's definitely something fishy going on up to the northwest of Junction 3. I took a little drive up that way on my way back from J4."

"What kind of fishy?"

"I'm not sure, but I think it's tied in somehow to the body that I found."

"And lost," Gaeretts commented wryly. As much as he liked the constable, he couldn't help making the dig.

"Well, I've found it again," Ortiz retorted.

There was a pause, then, "Could you repeat that, constable."

"I found my body again, Sergeant. It had been buried in a shallow grave about eighty kilometers north of the road. That's one of the reasons I'm reporting so late. I had to dig him up."

"You're sure it's the same body, Ortiz?" Gaeretts asked skeptically. "You aren't going to make a habit of finding dead people, are you?"

"It's the same body. I've got an ID on it, too. Or at least I think I do. There was an ID card in one of the outside pockets. The name on it was Ian Bates."

"Could you repeat that, constable?" Gaeretts asked, suddenly all business.

"Ian Bates," Elena repeated, puzzled. "Why? Does that name mean something to you?"

"It means something to the chief, Ortiz. McKernan has been looking into the activities of Bates and three of his buddies. He'll be real interested to hear what you have to say. He's not here now, but I'd expect him to give you a call back as soon as I let him know you've checked in. Where are you now?"

"I'm still on the road. Driving home. I should be there in a little over an hour."

"Where's your body?"

"It's strapped into one of the storage racks of the buggy. I wasn't about to make the mistake of leaving it behind a second time."

"Smart move. Well, drive safe."

"There is one other thing, sarge."

"What's that, constable?"

"I'm going to need a repair authorization on the buggy."

"What did you do? Hit a rock?"

"No. Someone took a shot at me. Put a hole in the front view port."

"Are you alright, Elena?" Gaeretts asked, sounding concerned.

"I'm fine. It was a shot from long range. I think it might have been more to scare me than anything else."

"The chief will have to hear about this, Elena. And don't do anything crazy until you hear from either me or the inspector. Do you understand?"

"I understand, sergeant."

"Good. I've got to try and get a hold of McKernan now. I'll talk to you later."

CHAPTER 22

It took them until late in the afternoon to complete the search of the hut, and even then, they hadn't found what McKernan was looking for. They had started with the kitchen area, checking each container and food pack. Fortunately, there hadn't been many of those, and the seals on the packs were unbroken. Fifteen minutes later, the inspector was convinced that nothing had been hidden in the cooking supplies.

After that the two of them had methodically worked their way towards the back of the hut, sifting through all the rubbish that had been allowed to accumulate. Bates and his roommates hadn't been neat or organized. Items of clothing had just been left lying around wherever they had been taken off. There was a big bag of unwashed clothing waiting to be laundered. Each item had to be examined in turn. Some of the items had labels sewn inside. In addition to Bates's name, the labels also included Stanton's and Martin's.

After an hour, they had lifted up each of the mattresses, examined every bit of trash, and opened or unscrewed the lid of every box, container, and jar without finding anything that looked remotely like it might be a drug.

After searching through the loose items, it was time to search for hiding places. A hut has a lot of them. Beneath the panels of the floor was a space that contained tanks for air and water as well as storage batteries for emergency power. Each panel had to be taken up and the space below checked. That took a couple of hours. Checking above the false ceiling took another. All they had found there was dust.

Everything that could be moved had been moved, and everything that could be opened had been opened. Mckernan was starting to wonder if the occupants had cleared out for good, and if they had taken whatever supplies of the drug they had with them.

"What do we do now, sir?" Ferris asked as he sat on a box and tried to brush the dust off of him.

McKernan gave him a smile. "You've got me, constable. I'm out of ideas as to where they could have hidden anything. We might as well pack it in. Thanks for your efforts, though. At the least I owe you a beer."

Ferris grinned. Getting praise from the chief inspector meant a lot. "I thought I saw a couple of beers in the cooler."

The constable got up and opened the door of the refrigerator, and was reaching in when McKernan interrupted, saying, "Ferris, you're a genius. Let me look at those bottles."

Ferris passed a bottle to the inspector, and then getting the idea took the other and started examining it.

It was a brand that was brewed and bottled locally for sale in company exchanges. It was a standard half liter plastic bottle with a screw off top that didn't require an opener. The plastic was a dark green that was almost opaque.

"Does this top look to you like it's been taken off and then screwed back on, constable?"

"Maybe. It's hard to tell."

"There's one way to find out. See if you can round up a clean container of some kind that we can pour the contents into."

Ferris came back in a few moments with a one liter measuring cup. McKernan unscrewed the cap of the bottle in his hands. There wasn't any sound of escaping gas.

"It seems to be flat," McKernan commented.

He started to pour the bottle into the measuring cup. The liquid that came out, whatever it was, certainly wasn't beer. It was clear. McKernan gave it a sniff, but it didn't have any odor. Tentatively he dipped a finger tip into it and gave a taste.

"Water," he announced to Ferris.

As he continued to pour a string of small capsules popped out of the mouth of the bottle into the cup. When the last drop had been poured he counted twenty capsules floating around. The capsules were clear and about the size used for dispensing cold medicine back on Earth.

"Do you want me to open the other bottle, sir?"

"No, let's keep that one intact as evidence. And see if there's a container in the forensics kit to put this stuff in. I think we're done here. Let's pack up and get out of here. I believe I promised you a beer, Ferris, and I mean to keep my promise."

The constable packed up the forensics kit. There didn't seem much point in cleaning up the hut. On the way out, McKernan slapped a seal on the airlock hatch and a "crime scene" sticker on the door. He didn't know how long that would be effective in keeping out scavengers, but he didn't really care. He was pretty certain that he'd found what he'd come for.

Fifteen minutes later, they were standing at the bar in Finnegan's where the inspector kept his promise.

"Can I buy you another round, sir?" Ferris said as he finished the last of his beer.

"Thanks, but I'll have to take a rain check on that, constable. I want to get this sample to Dr. Greenwood to analyze. But feel free to have another. We did good work today."

It was past 1700, but the nurse at the reception desk told him that Dr. Greenwood was still in the hospital when McKernan asked for him. She opened the door to the surgery to let him through and then returned her attention to her computer.

If Greenwood was surprised when he looked up to see the inspector, he didn't show it.

"I've got something I'd like you to analyze for me, doc," McKernan said dropping the evidence container on the lab table. "It's connected to that business we were talking about the other day."

"Way Back?" Greenwood asked, suddenly interested.

"Yes. I think I know who's been making it, and I think I've got some samples of it here. I'm pretty sure you can ignore the liquid. Just look at the capsules."

The doctor used a pair of tweezers to fish the capsules out of the container and laid them on a clean sheet of filter paper. When he had removed the last of them he place one of the capsules on the stage of a microscope.

"Standard gel cap. Easy enough to get. Looks like it may have been filled locally rather than in a factory on Earth. What makes you think this might be Way Back?"

"I found the capsules hidden in a beer bottle in an abandoned place out at the end of Hut Town. The person who's been living there has a friend named Jeremy Stanton. The liquid in the container was from the bottle. I'm pretty sure it isn't beer."

Greenwood raised an eyebrow.

"Can I open one or two of these up?" he said indicating the capsules. "I'll have to destroy the contents in the process."

"That's what I'm here for, doc," McKernan said.

"This is going to take awhile."

"I can wait. I just spent all afternoon searching for those. A few more minutes won't be a problem."

The doctor spent the next few minutes preparing some samples for several tests. The laboratory wasn't equipped anywhere near as well as it would have been on Earth, but it did have several expensive pieces of apparatus including a mass spectrograph and a gas chromatograph.

When Greenwood was done with his preparations and had started his tests he said, "It will take a few minutes to get the results. Can I offer you a drink while we wait?"

"I wouldn't say no," McKernan responded.

Greenwood opened one of the lower drawers in the lab table and pulled out what McKernan recognized as a very good bottle of single malt. The doctor poured a few fingers into a pair of beakers and handed one to the inspector.

"There's water over there if you want to add a splash." McKernan noted that the doctor didn't add any to his own beaker.

They drank in silence. After a few moments, the doctor checked on his apparatus, but seemed satisfied that the tests were proceeding smoothly.

"Have you given much thought to what's going to happen?" the doctor asked.

"I'm not sure I follow you, doc."

"I'm talking about what's going to happen after this election."

"I'm not sure that much *is* going to happen. At least in the short term," McKernan replied.

"But what about the longer term? Let's face it McKernan, both of us have been on Mars a long time. Neither one of us has been planning on ever going back. But we're both employees of the Trust Authority. If home rule takes effect, will there still be a place on Mars for people like us?"

"I guess we're Martians as much as anyone."

"But will everyone else see it that way?" Greenwood asked.

"I wouldn't be too worried, doc. Mars is still going to need doctors no matter who is running the place. And it's not like it's going to grow its own any time soon."

Greenwood took a sip of his drink. "Maybe you're right about that, McKernan. Maybe people will act sensibly. There's always a first time. What about you? What are your plans?"

"I haven't thought much past the election. I guess I'll just keep hanging on until someone tells me I don't have a paycheck coming in. If that happens, I'll probably try to find something else. Maybe work security for one of the companies. I know a few people and have a few favors to call in if it comes to that."

"What is Beth thinking of doing?" Greenwood asked thoughtfully.

McKernan was relieved from having to answer that question by a beeping that came from the mass spectrometer indicating that the analysis was done. Greenwood got up to check the device's display, checking it against some information he brought up on a computer tablet.

"Don't keep me in suspense, doc."

"Analyzing a complex organic is never that simple or as cut and dried as saying that something contains arsenic or not. But given what I know about the drug, the results are consistent with the contents of the capsule being Way Back. Within the limits of this lab, that's about as much as I can tell you. We can send a sample back to Earth if you want something more definitive."

"Maybe later. You've given me enough to go on for the moment. I'd appreciate a written report on your results when you get a chance, but there's no rush. Thanks, doc. And thanks for the Scotch."

McKernan drained what was left in the beaker and left.

Gaeretts was behind the desk at the security station when McKernan got there. The sergeant had a concerned look on his face.

"I just heard from Constable Ortiz, chief."

"What's up?"

"Elena's been doing some poking around up north of the road in relation to that missing body of hers. It's not missing anymore. She found it buried in a shallow grave. She dug it up and is bringing it back to Junction 3. She found an ID card on the victim. It belonged to Ian Bates."

"Bates?"

"Yeah. I thought that would get your attention. There was one other thing. She said that someone took a shot at her."

"Is she OK?" McKernan said, alarmed.

"That's what she says, and I suspect we have to trust our girl. But things are getting serious."

"Yeah. I just came from Doc Greenwood. He analyzed some of the capsules that we found in the hut. He says they are consistent with it being Way Back. He won't commit to more than that without sending some back to Earth, but for now I'll take his word on it."

"Thinks are breaking quickly, aren't they, chief?"

"Yeah, they are. Look, tell Elena to hold at Junction 3 until she hears from me. Under no circumstances is she to act on her own. And you might get on the phone to Kaminski and tell him to head towards J4 in the morning. I may need him as backup."

"You're going out there?"

"That seems to be where things are headed. I'll be in my office. I've got to see what I can arrange as far as transportation."

CHAPTER 23

The rest of Elena's drive home to Junction 3 passed without incident. Driving in the dark on Mars was never much fun. It was easy to lose your references and there was never any moonlight to light up the landscape. Fortunately, the road was well marked and well enough traveled that there had been little danger of Elena losing her way.

Still, caution had dictated that she keep her speed down, and it had taken her nearly two hours to cover the last eighty kilometers. She was glad when the lights of Junction 3 came into view. She noticed that there were more of them on than usual. Mike had probably had the place lit up just for her.

She pulled the buggy up in front of the garage and turned off the motor. She hadn't realized how tired she was, but then she'd been driving since 0600. She ached from head to toe, and all she wanted to do was take a shower and get between some clean sheets.

She was still running through the shutdown check list when she saw the figure in the surface suit approaching. From the markings on the suit, she recognized it as Mike. She wasn't surprised that he had been waiting for her or that he had suited up to do so.

"Honey, I'm home," she called over the suit radio.

"So I noticed," Mike said. The tenseness in his voice came through the radio. She saw that he was looking at the point where the bullet had pierced the front viewport. She could almost see him do the mental calculations of the trajectory.

"What were you thinking, Elena? What if he hadn't missed?"

"I wasn't expecting anyone to be there, Mike. I certainly wasn't expecting someone to take a pot shot at me."

It had been a reasonable expectation. Theoretically, firearms were limited to the security service, and no one else was allowed to possess or import either weapons or ammunition. The prohibition wasn't completely foolproof, but instances where it had been broken could be numbered on the fingers of one hand.

"Still, you shouldn't have been out there alone, Elena."

"And who would back me up. Kaminski is the nearest and he's a thousand kilometers away. But you don't have to worry, Mike. McKernan has ordered me to sit tight until he gets here."

She realized the wisdom of the chief inspector's orders, but she couldn't help resenting that the case was being taken away from her.

She cycled through the buggy's airlock. There was an awkward embrace with Mike as she stepped down onto the ground. Surface suits had never been intended for intimacy.

"There's something that I've got to take care of," Elena said after a moment. She pointed at the body in the storage rack on the side of the buggy. "Is there someplace safe that we can stash it? After what happened the last time, I don't want to take any chances on it disappearing on me again."

"There's the storage shed in back. It's got a padlock on the door. It's not pressurized, but I assume that doesn't matter."

Elena shook her head, and then realizing that Mike might not see the gesture she said, "No. The body has already been exposed. I just want to keep it intact until we can put it on the road train to Mars City."

Moving the body was easier with Mike to help her, but bodies are awkward things to carry, especially when in a surface suit. Even with the lower gravity, Elena was sweating by the time they got the body in the shed. She could tell that Mike was breathing heavily, too.

There was an airlock in the back of the garage so that they didn't have to go around to the front to get in. Inside, Mike helped her out of her surface suit. She didn't resist. She didn't resist when he kissed her, either, though she would rather just have gone to bed.

Finally, she said, "There's something I want you to take a look at."

Mike looked at her curiously. Elena fumbled around in a pocket of her surface suit and pulled out an evidence bag. Inside was the fragment that she had pried out of the wall of the buggy.

Mike took the bag and held it up to the light, examining it with a practiced eye.

"Is this what came through the viewport?"

"Yes. I found it in the back wall of the buggy. It must have had an almost flat trajectory. There wasn't any nearby cover and I sure as hell didn't spot the shooter. He must have been a kilometer away or more."

"This isn't a normal rifle round," Mike said.

"That's what I thought, too. Any idea of what kind of weapon it came from?"

"Let me check something," Mike said. He went into the shop and came back with a caliper. He popped the bullet out of the pouch and measured it.

"Fourteen millimeters. Bigger than a .50 caliber. I don't think this came from a commercial round. My guess is that it's homemade. The weapon probably was homemade, too.

More than likely, a single shot bolt action. Almost like an old style buffalo rifle."

"How hard would it be to make something like that?"

"It would be a lot of work, and you'd have to really know what you were doing, but with the right tools, it wouldn't be impossible. The ammunition would be harder, but looking at it, I'd say that bullet was machined and not cast."

"But how accurate would something like that be? As I said, he must have been over a kilometer away when he fired."

"That kind of accuracy wouldn't be a problem. See the scratches on the bullet. That came from rifling in the barrel. Gives the bullet a spin to stabilize it. And with no windage to speak of, all the shooter would really have to worry about would be the drop due to gravity, and that would be easy to figure out based on the distance. Some of the old buffalo guns were good to a mile or more."

"Great."

"Count yourself lucky. The bullet was traveling so fast it just punched a hole through the viewport. If it had been going slower, the window might have shattered on you."

"You're just full of cheery info. Let's talk about it tomorrow. Right now I'm tired, Mike. I haven't had anything to eat since noon and I just want to go to bed."

"There's some soup in the kitchen. I'll warm it up for you."

"That sounds great, Mike. What about Miguel?"

"I put him to bed. He wanted to wait up for you, but he fell asleep."

"I'll go and look in on him while you warm the soup."

Miguel was asleep when she went into his room, but he woke enough to smile at her before falling back to sleep. Elena was glad to be home.

In the kitchen, Mike had poured a bowl of soup for her and set it on the table. It had potatoes and carrots and pieces of ham floating in it, spiced with paprika. Elena thought it smelled incredible. There was a slice of bread and a glass of wine, too. Mike had poured a glass for himself as well, though he'd eaten earlier.

He didn't say much while she ate. That was one of the things she liked about him, he didn't talk when he didn't need to.

After she had finished the soup and half the wine, the constable got out her tablet to check for messages.

"McKernan says he's coming tomorrow if he can arrange a plane," she told Mike after she had read the message.

"So you're going after this guy?" Mike asked.

"Yeah. It seems that the inspector thinks the body I found ties in with a case he's been working on. Some guys have been making a drug that causes people to forget that they're on Mars."

"That doesn't sound safe," Mike said uncertainly.

"It isn't. I think that's what happened to the guy out in the shed. He forgot that he was on Mars and was wondering why he had a helmet on. So he opened up the faceplate."

"But, from what you were saying, wasn't he one of the people making this drug?"

"Yeah. Makes you wonder, doesn't it?"

"It just seems crazy," Mike said shaking his head.

"You've got that right. Look, I'm tired, Mike. Let's go to bed."

Mike fell asleep with his arm around her, but Elena lay awake a long time thinking about the body in the dust.

CHAPTER 24

Junction 3 was roughly fifteen hundred kilometers from Mars City. Even driving straight through, McKernan knew it would take the better part of two days just to reach the outpost and another day to drive north to the point where Ortiz had been shot at. It was time that he didn't want to waste.

There were only two other possibilities available to him, and only one was realistic. Theoretically, one of the shuttles used to reach ships in orbit would be capable of taking off from the port and setting down at Junction 3, but the problem with that was that there was no way his budget would stretch to a dedicated launch. The other alternative was one of the rocket planes that had been specially designed to work in the low gravity and air pressure of Mars.

His department didn't have one of these planes. Even the U.N. Trust Authority didn't own one, but the larger mining companies maintained a small fleet that was used mostly for shuttling executives and high value cargo around. Though McKernan was a qualified pilot, he knew he had a better chance of hitching a ride than requisitioning a plane.

He placed a call to Andrew Fletcher, the Chief of Operations at the spaceport. Luckily, he was still in his office to answer the call.

"Inspector, what can I do for you?" the chief answered in a heavy Yorkshire accent.

"I need to get to Junction 3 as soon as possible. It's a priority situation."

"Like that, is it, Erik?" Fletcher asked.

"Yeah. I'd appreciate it if you'd keep this under your hat, but someone took a pot shot at Constable Ortiz out that way and she needs some backup."

"Aye. Sounds serious. I'm afraid I haven't a loaner at the moment. A couple of ships are down for maintenance. Sorry about that."

"I understand, Andy. Is there anything headed out in that direction that I could bum a ride on?"

"Nothing tonight if you're in a real hurry?"

McKernan wasn't surprised. No one flew at night on Mars if they could help it. "I just want to get there quicker than I can drive it."

"Anglo-Martian has got a flight scheduled in the morning for their mining camp north of Junction 4. I suppose they might drop you off at Junction 3 on the way. They've got a landing strip there and they can top off the tanks to make up for the fuel and oxidizer consumed on the extra landing and takeoff. If you'll pay for it, that is?"

"Considering the situation, I think I can stretch my budget that far."

"The plane is at the weight limit right now. I'll have to take some of the cargo off to make room for you, but I can manage as long as you keep your mass under a hundred kilos."

"Do you want me to clear it with Otis," McKernan asked, referring to Otis McAndrews the head of Anglo-Martian.

"No need to be troubling the old man," Fletcher replied. "I'll take you at your word that this is serious."

"Thanks, Andy."

"Take off is scheduled for 0800, but I might be able to push that up a bit. Get you to Junction 3 by say 1100 or so."

"Sounds good, Andy. Expect me by 0700."

"I'll be waiting."

"Thanks, again."

McKernan had called Beth to tell her that he'd be late and not to wait dinner on him. She had eaten, but was still up when he reached the hut.

"Sorry that I'm late. Something came up." Both of their jobs were such that they were used to irregular schedules.

"It's not a problem. I wasn't sure when you'd be home so I ate earlier, but there's still some dinner left in the pressure cooker if you're hungry."

He went over to the small kitchen area and turned up the cooker to reheat the contents. He didn't even bother to check what was inside.

"Was it the drug case?" Beth asked as he got a plate and silverware ready.

"Yeah, that and the fact that someone took a shot at Elena."

"Is she alright?" Beth asked with concern. Despite the fact that they lived fifteen hundred kilometers apart, the two women had formed a bond during Elena's pregnancy with Miguel.

"She's fine. The shot missed, but I'm flying out there tomorrow to help track down whoever did it."

"Why would anyone want to shoot Elena?" Beth asked.

"Elena was poking her nose in things up north of the road. Evidently somebody didn't like that," Erik answered laconically

"Do you think it has something to do with that body she found?"

"It's looking that way. By the way, she's found the body again. Somebody had buried it. We think we know who it is now, too. Ian Bates."

"That's one of the men you think was involved with your drug case, isn't it?"

"Yup—" McKernan was interrupted by the beeping of the timer on the pressure cooker. He opened the lid, used his finger to check the temperature of the contents, and then began spooning them, a stew of rice, vegetables and chicken onto his plate.

"Do you want some wine?" Beth asked. She sounded more interested than concerned.

"That sounds good," McKernan said as he set the plate down at the dining table.

McKernan took a few bitefuls, and then continued, "We can't really be sure yet, but from the build of the body it looks like a pretty good match. And no one has seen Bates in some time. Now that Elena has found her body again, we'll be able to make sure it's him."

Beth set down a glass of wine next to Erik and then took the other chair at the table. "And you think he's connected to this drug ring?"

"Yeah. We raided a place at the far end of Hut Town that the four were using when they were in town. No one was home, but during the search we uncovered what I think is some Way Back. There were two or three dozen homemade capsules hidden in a couple of beer bottles in the refrigerator suspended in water so that the capsules wouldn't rattle if you shook the bottle. Pretty clever actually, but then these are some pretty smart boys.

"I think that Elena must have come close to stumbling on where they've been growing the plants to make the drug. Someone took a shot at her to discourage her. At least I'm hoping they were just trying to scare her off and not kill her. That's why I have to go out there tomorrow."

Concern crossed Beth's face. "This sounds dangerous, Erik."

"Maybe. I'm hoping that these guys aren't really the violent type. There's nothing to indicate that Bates' death was anything except an accident. I halfway suspect that he took too much of his own drug and forgot he was on Mars. He opened the faceplate on his helmet, and that was that. The other three found him sometime after Elena had, panicked, and they moved the body and then later buried it where Elena found it the second time."

"Maybe that's all true, but be careful, Erik. I don't want to lose you. Not now."

The inspector looked up. Beth had expressed her concern about the dangers of his work before, but this was something different.

"Don't worry. I'll be careful. Besides, it won't be just me. There will be three of us. I'm having Kaminski meet us on the way in addition to Ortiz, so we'll have plenty of firepower on hand."

In the morning, McKernan got up before Beth. He had a shower and a quick breakfast. He stopped at the station to pick up the surface suit that he kept there. Gaeretts was already there. The inspector suspected that he slept at the station half of the time.

As McKernan unlocked the weapons locker and grabbed one of the carbines from the rack the sergeant remarked, "Going loaded for bear are we?"

"I need something with some range. From what you told me, the shot at Elena was taken from a kilometer or more away. I want to be able to shoot back."

Gaeretts just grunted. He didn't comment either, when McKernan took the .44 revolver out of its case and slipped it into the bag he had with him.

"Kaminski is on his way to J4. He started early and should get there by the time you land at J3," Gaeretts said as McKernan shut the locker.

"Good. I'll call you when I land."

It was just turning 0700 when McKernan walked into the operations shack at the spaceport. Fletcher was waiting for him along with the pilot and four passengers. McKernan knew the pilot and recognized three of the passengers.

"Let's get you weighed in, Inspector," Fletcher said.

McKernan stood on the scale along with the bag containing his surface suit and the carbine case.

"Ninety-nine kilos. Cutting it close, but I won't have to toss anything else off the plane. Are you ready?"

"I'm ready when you are, gentlemen."

CHAPTER 25

When Elena woke up, she discovered that Mike had risen before her. After the long drive she had been dead tired, and she appreciated the extra time nestled in bed. She reached over to grab her comm and checked for messages. There was one from McKernan saying that he would be arriving by plane sometime around 1100. It was only 0820 so that gave her time for a leisurely breakfast.

After she had dressed, she found Miguel playing quietly in the small space that served as their living room.

"Good morning, Miguel. Did Daddy fix you breakfast?"

"No. He said you would when you got up. He said I should be quiet and let you sleep. Are you done sleeping, Mommy?"

"I'm done sleeping. Let's see what we can make for breakfast."

Her schedule didn't give her time for domestic tasks very often, so Elena took the opportunity to make Miguel and herself a batch of pancakes. The bacon she fried up to go with them had come from one of the hogs Jenny's husband raised in the farm behind the station, but the butter and sugar were expensive imports from Earth. Mars didn't have much of a dairy industry yet.

As she cleaned up the kitchen after breakfast, Elena thought again what a strange childhood it was for Miguel, growing up in a place where he would never be able to go outside without wearing a surface suit. There weren't many kids his age on Mars, either. Miguel had been one of the first children born on Mars, though Jenny had a girl just a year younger than Miguel and another one on the way. Still, she knew that if she had remained in Brownsville, the prospects for any children she had would have probably been pretty bleak. That was one of the reasons she had joined the Air Force right out of high school. She had wanted to rise in life. She just hadn't imagined that it would have been so far.

She took her time getting ready, but finally she went out to the shop. She wanted to be ready when the chief inspector showed up. As bosses went, McKernan was a good one, but, perhaps because of that, she didn't want to disappoint him.

Mike had pulled her buggy into one of the pressurized equipment bays and was working on the front viewport. He had removed her temporary patch and was replacing it with something more durable.

"I'd prefer to replace the whole panel," Mike said when he saw her, "but I don't have a salvaged one available. I'd have to get one from Mars City, and I'm guessing that I don't have time for that."

"McKernan sent me a message that he'll be landing here sometime around 1100. We'll probably be heading out later today."

"I'd better get this finished up then," Mike said tersely. He didn't much mind her driving patrol, that was about as safe as anything was on Mars, but she knew that her facing anything more dangerous made him uneasy.

"Someone's got to do it, Mike. We can't let someone go around taking pot shots at people. Besides, McKernan will be with me. You know that he'll be the one taking all the risks." The chief inspector had a reputation that wasn't exaggerated. "And Kaminski will be meeting up with us before we have a confrontation."

"Well, just take care of yourself, Elena."

"I will, Mike. I promise. I'd better get suited up so I'm ready to meet the inspector when he lands."

Planes rarely landed at Junction 3. Most people arriving or leaving used the road train or buggies. For emergencies, a landing strip had been carved out of the Martian landscape, though that mostly had meant using a grader to level out a space twenty meters wide and a kilometer and a half long and then removing the larger rocks. It made for rough landings, but then, any plane designed for Mars had to be built for such conditions.

The plane radioed ahead when it got near, and by the time Elena had gone through the airlock, she could spot it making its approach. She stood well clear of the landing strip as she waited for it to land.

It always amazed her that the things could fly at all in the thin Martian atmosphere. With a huge wingspan that owed more to the high-altitude spy planes of the 1950's than anything else, the plane looked much too fragile to be carrying human cargo. The pilot knew his stuff, though, touching down not far from the markers at the end of the strip and skidding on its skis in a great spray of dust. It came to rest well short of the half-way point of the runway.

Mike was already in the buggy that had been converted into a fueling truck. As the cockpit of the buggy was an open one, Elena hopped into the passenger seat and they drove out to meet the plane. McKernan was just climbing out of the belly airlock when they pulled up.

"Constable," McKernan greeted her tersely.

"Sir," Elena responded.

"OK, we've got the formalities out of the way. How's Miguel? Beth would never forgive me if I didn't ask."

"He's fine, sir. He had pancakes for breakfast."

"He's doing better than I did," McKernan grinned.

While they were talking, Mike had hooked up the fueling hose to top off the tanks of the plane. Takeoffs used a lot of fuel, and pilots didn't like to take the chance of running low. McKernan and Ortiz stood by during this process which didn't take five minutes. When the hoses were disconnected, they got in the buggy, and drove away from the plane. They hadn't gotten more than a hundred meters when the twin engines of the plane fired up. A minute later the plane started to move, quickly gained speed and then leapt into the air. It had spent less than ten minutes on the ground.

"He was sure in a hurry," Mike said over the suit intercom.

"I threw his schedule off by hitching a ride and having him drop me off here," McKernan explained. "You didn't have to come out to meet me, Elena."

"I've got something to show you, sir. We've got it locked up in a shed outside."

McKernan didn't respond.

Mike pulled the tanker up next to the shed. After stopping the engine, he got out. He made a show of unlocking the shed but didn't say anything. McKernan took a look inside.

"So, your body didn't walk away from you this time."

"I thought it best not to bring him inside," Elena said.

"You're probably right. No sense letting it decompose, and after laying outside for a few days, it's not going to be in any worse condition."

McKernan took a good look at body, noting details of the suit and making a close study of the face.

"Not a particularly pretty sight, but I'm satisfied that that was Ian Bates. I'd say that the cause of death is just what you said it was, too, Elena. It looks like he just opened up the faceplate of his helmet. There aren't any other marks on the suit, and no signs of any trauma other than from decompression."

"Not a good way to go," Mike commented.

"No, it isn't," the inspector agreed.

"Why would anyone do that?" Elena asked.

"My guess is that he just didn't realize that he was on Mars anymore."

"That drug you've been looking into?" Elena queried.

"Yeah. I think this guy," McKernan said indicating the corpse, "and his three buddies have been making it in a hideout they have up north of here. That's why they took a pot shot at you, constable. You were getting too close. You might as well lock it up again, Mike. I'll want it sent in to Mars City on the next road train, but until then it might as well sit out here as anywhere."

Mike relocked the shed door.

"I'd like to get out to the place where you found the body while there's still enough light to look around. Kaminski is going to meet us at the coordinates you gave in you report. Do you have a buggy ready to go?"

"I patched up the hole in the viewport in Elena's and checked over everything else this morning, inspector," Mike answered. "She's ready to go whenever you want it."

"Good."

They headed to the garage airlock which was large enough to hold the three of them. Once inside, they were able to take off their helmets. Mike led the way to the garage bay where Elena's buggy stood, the U.N. Trust Authority logo prominent on its sides.

"Before we go, there's something else I want to show you," Elena said.

"What's that?"

"I've got the slug that came through the window. I thought you might like to have an idea of what we're going to be up against."

She produced the evidence bag containing the piece of metal she'd found. "I dug this out of a plastic compartment cover at the back of buggy. The plastic must have absorbed a lot of the momentum and left it pretty much intact."

McKernan took the bag and held it up to the light to get a better look at the sharply pointed cylinder.

"I'm not sure I've ever seen a bullet like this before. Any ideas as to what it came from?"

Mike chimed in, "I measured the diameter as 14 millimeters. That's a lot bigger than the standard automatic rifle rounds the security forces use. Bigger than any handgun rounds, too, at least that I know of."

"Bigger than anything I know of, either, at least on Mars. 14 millimeters is almost a cannon. You think that it might be from some sort of sniper rifle or big game gun?"

Mike shook his head. "I think it was probably homemade. That slug looks like it was machined out of steel rather than molded or forged. My guess is that the rifle was probably homemade as well."

It was clear to McKernan that Mike had been thinking a lot about the weapon. He saw no reason not to let him go on. "You think that's possible?"

"I could probably make one myself if I had enough time on my hands and the right tools. A rifle is really nothing more than a tube that's sealed at one end. If you make it bolt-action and single shot, it would be pretty simple, really. Use electricity to set it off rather than a firing pin, and the trigger wouldn't have to be very complicated, either, just a switch."

"Any idea of the range? McKernan asked.

"Judging from the hole in the viewport and where I dug the slug out, it was almost a level trajectory," Elena remarked. "I couldn't spot the shooter, and the nearest cover was more than a kilometer away."

"It was still moving pretty fast when it hit the viewport," Mike added. "It went right through rather than shattering it, which it might have done if it was going slower."

"And with no atmosphere to speak of or wind to worry about it could be pretty accurate at that kind of distance."

"I'm pretty sure the barrel was rifled to impart spin," Mike said.

"Not particularly comforting," McKernan responded, "but it's good to know what we're up against. Well, if you're ready to go, Elena, we should get moving. I'd like to reach the spot where you found the body while we still have light. I'd just as soon get there before Kaminski does. I don't want him to be a sitting duck by himself."

"I'm ready to go as soon as we get our gear stowed."

"We might as well get going, then."

Elena went through the buggy's airlock first. As McKernan was waiting his turn, Mike said, "Inspector, try to keep Elena safe."

"Don't worry, Mike. I won't let anything happen to the constable."

CHAPTER 26

McKernan had no problem with letting Ortiz drive the buggy. She was familiar with the route and, having spent countless hours driving patrol, there was no question that the constable had a lot more experience. It occurred to the inspector that he had spent relatively little of the past few years out on the surface of Mars. His duties had mostly kept him within the fused glass walls of Mars City or the pressurized corridors of Hut Town.

Taking advantage of the circumstances, he spent the first few hours of the drive just taking in the Martian landscape as it passed by. This was by no means the most scenic or dramatic part of Mars, but it still possessed a kind of stark beauty similar to, yet different than, that of parts of western North America or Australia. He felt an urge to have Ortiz stop the buggy so that he could get out and experience the sand and rocks at first hand, but he also knew, that even if the Green party were allowed to go ahead with their plans for terraforming, never in his lifetime would he be able to do so without the protection of a surface suit.

As they drove, McKernan couldn't help but keep eyeing the patch in the front bubble of the buggy. He knew Mike's reputation as a craftsman well enough not to say anything. The mechanic would never risk Elena's life with a shoddy repair, but, as a Martian, anything that might compromise pressure integrity made him nervous. It was just an ingrained instinct, the kind of instinct that kept you alive.

Elena, for her part, was content to drive in silence. She had worked several cases with the Chief Inspector and considered him a friend, but she also knew that he kept his thoughts to himself. Most of the time she drove alone, so the lack of conversation didn't bother her.

Driving in the middle of the day along a well traveled portion of the road, they were able to make good time. It wasn't long after 1300 that she announced, "This is where we turn off, sir."

"How far to the spot where you found your body?"

"About a hundred kilometers. We should be able to get there in three hours."

"Good, that should give us plenty of light to check it out."

As Elena turned off the road and headed towards the pass, she could see the tracks that she had made the previous day.

McKernan said, "I'm going to see where Kaminski is. If he's close enough, we'll wait for him to catch up to us."

After raising Kaminski on his comm, McKernan discovered that the constable was still some forty minutes from the turnoff. The inspector decided to press on and have Kaminski follow their tracks north.

As they drove, he studied the images that Ortiz had found showing activity. He followed the track as it led north until it stopped. The terrain was pretty rough. The tracks ended on the lower part of the slope of an ancient shield volcano. There weren't any signs of man-made structures visible on the surface, though there were plenty of vehicle tracks or at least what looked like vehicle tracks. Curiously, some of them appeared to disappear into the hillside.

Could the installation be underground? That seemed unlikely. Excavating such a facility would require an enormous amount of work. Still, he wondered, why all the signs of activity if there was nothing there?

After driving for an hour and going through the pass, they stopped for a brief break. McKernan offered to take over the driving, but Ortiz said that she was fine. The inspector didn't press the point. Instead, he broke out the binoculars and started to scan the landscape ahead of them. They were still far from where Ortiz had been ambushed, but he didn't want to be caught off guard.

They reached the marker just after 1600. McKernan had the buggy stop a hundred meters short so as not to disturb the tracks Ortiz had made the previous night.

Neither of them had taken off their surface suits while they were driving. Now they put on their helmets and went through the checkout list for their life support packs. McKernan uncased the semi-automatic carbine that he had brought with him. The inspector smiled to himself when he saw that Ortiz had armed herself with a riot gun. The shotgun would be useless at long range, but close in against someone in a surface suit it would be deadly.

"Should I bring the evidence kit, sir?"

"Might as well. I don't know if we'll find anything, but at least I want to take images of the site and anything else that looks interesting. I'll go first."

The buggy's airlock was only big enough for one person to exit at a time. McKernan stepped in, let the lock cycle, and then stepped down onto the surface. He kept the carbine at the ready as he scanned the hills around them.

Ortiz emerged from the airlock a moment later. She had the riot gun slung over one shoulder and the evidence kit slung over the other. McKernan didn't seem to notice.

As they walked towards the marker, Elena pointed out the tracks of her buggy both coming and going. There were other tracks as well. It looked as if two buggies had been traveling in line. It was always hard to judge how old tracks were on Mars. In the low atmospheric pressure, tracks could remain for years. These tracks, though, looked fresh and they appeared to be heading north.

"I didn't notice those before, sir. But it was late and the light was pretty bad."

"That's why I wanted to get here while the sun was still up. It looks to me like one buggy following another. They stopped here, and someone got out from each buggy," McKernan said, pointing at the footprints. "They were dragging something, too. Looks like your body. Get some pictures of the prints."

They followed the footprints towards the marker. Ortiz's efforts to dig up the body had erased some of them, but it was clear that they had approached the marker and then gone no further.

"I'm afraid I made kind of a mess of things trying to recover the body, sir."

"Not much else you could have done under the circumstances, constable. I doubt that anything useful in the way of evidence got disturbed. Given the wandering habits of your corpse, it was better to get it under lock and key then leave it. Take some more photos, anyway."

"Why do you think they did it, sir? I mean, bury the body, but then put up a marker?"

"I think they put up the marker because the dead man was a friend. They weren't trying to hide the body as much as trying to keep it from pointing at them. They must have thought that this place was far enough out of the way that no one would stumble upon it, and even if someone did it wouldn't lead to them. They hadn't factored in your looking through a mass of satellite imagery to find their trail."

"So what do we do now, sir?"

"I think we've done as much as we can here. As soon as Kaminski catches up we should head north. If your guess from the imagery is right, we've got six or seven hours of driving to get there. I'd like to do as much of that as we can before it gets dark."

They didn't have long to wait. Kaminski's buggy appeared twenty minutes later. After a brief discussion, they headed north again.

Three hours later, McKernan called a halt as the sun was about to set. They found an outcrop that provided them some protection from being seen, and pulled the two buggies up adjacent to each other. Kaminski suited up and came over to the other vehicle for a consultation and dinner.

With three of them, the inside of Ortiz's buggy was cramped, but Elena and Kaminski were used to the tight quarters.

"What's for dinner?" Kaminski asked when he'd gotten settled. He hadn't bothered to take off his surface suit, though he had removed the life support pack and helmet.

"I've got rice, beans, and chicken or rice, beans, and ham," Elena said rummaging around the food storage locker. "If you don't like either of those, I've got rice and beans."

"It figures," Kaminski complained.

"If you've got something better in your buggy, go get it," Elena countered. The exchange was good-natured; they had worked together long enough to build up trust and respect.

"Nothing worth suiting up for. I guess I'll take the rice, beans, and chicken."

"You, sir?" Elena asked.

"I'll take whatever you have the most of," McKernan answered.

"Rice, beans, and ham it is. I know it's not up to Mars City standards, sir, but I've got a bottle of hot sauce to spice it up." She handed the meal pouch to the inspector. "For drinks I've got grape, grape, or grape. I'm waiting on a new shipment of supplies."

"In that case, I'll take grape."

Ortiz tossed each of them one of the drink pouches before resuming her place in the driver's seat. Kaminski had folded down one of the jump seats and was waiting for his meal to heat itself.

The three of them ate in silence except for requests for the bottle of homemade hot sauce that Elena had produced.

When they had finished, and Elena had put the empty food packs in the trash compactor, she returned carrying a bottle that had been hidden in one of the storage compartments.

"Care for a little joy juice. Jenny's husband has been working on the formula. His latest batch isn't bad."

"I take it I'm not driving tonight?" Kaminski asked.

"No, we're parked for the night," McKernan answered.

"In that case--" Kaminski said as he held out his cup.

"You, sir?"

"Why not?"

After they had taken a few sips, McKernan asked, "Are you ready for the election?" Kaminski would be responsible for overseeing the voting at Junction Five, his home base.

"As ready as I can be. I'm not expecting more than a couple of dozen people to show up. Almost anyone who can is going to Mars City for the vote. Those that can't make it there are planning on heading to Junction 3.

Sounds like you're going to have a real shindig on your hands, Elena."

"Yeah. Jenny is laying in extra supplies for the occasion. There's going to be a real party after the vote, but people are still taking it seriously."

"We've had to break up a few fist fights in Mars City," McKernan commented. "Nothing serious, and they shook hands afterwards, but people are getting pretty excited about the whole thing, not that there is that much difference between the Reds and the Greens when you come right down to it."

"So where do you stand?" Elena asked.

"Me? I'm trying to stay neutral," the inspector said.

"I guess when I think about it, I side with the Reds," Kaminski said after taking a sip. "Mars is what it is. I don't see a good reason to go changing it. What about you, Elena?"

"I kind of like the idea of kids being able to go outside some day without a surface suit and a helmet. I know it's not going to happen in my lifetime or even Miguel's, but one day—" Elena said wistfully.

"Whoever wins, nothing much is going to happen in a hurry. Not if the U. N. is involved," McKernan stated.

"That's for sure. Anyone care for another?"

"Not for me," Kaminski replied. "I'd better get back to my buggy."

After he'd gone through the lock, Elena held up the bottle. "Sir?"

"No, I think that Kaminski has the right idea. We should all get some sleep. No telling what we're going to run into tomorrow."

CHAPTER 27

The two buggies were on the move as soon as there was enough light to drive by. Elena and McKernan were in the lead, with Elena doing the driving, though they were now well past the farthest point she had reached on her previous trip. She noticed that McKernan was scanning the high points, both with the naked eye and binoculars. She tried to divide her attention between the horizon and the terrain in front of her, but the ground they were covering was getting more difficult to drive through and she had to concentrate on that.

The farther north they got the more tense Elena felt, though she knew it was unlikely that someone would be watching for them until they got close to the site of the secret installation. She only had to glance at the repair Mike had made to the viewport to remind her of what they were up against.

There were plenty of buggy tracks to follow. Evidently the drug dealers had made numerous trips to their base, always following approximately the same route. Occasionally, Elena would lose the trail when they traversed a particularly hard patch of ground, but she never had any difficulty picking them up again.

They'd been driving for nearly four hours when McKernan called a halt. According to the satellite images they were only a few kilometers from their destination which was just over a low ridge.

Elena patched in Kaminski's radio so that the three of them could hold a conference. The inspector had brought up a topographical map of the area on the computer screen and was alternating looking at that and the satellite image of the spot that Elena had found. Kaminski had copies of both available to him on his own computer so that he could follow the discussion.

"I want us to go in from two different angles," McKernan said as he explained his plan. "Kaminski, I want you to take the left approach. There's a sort of depression leading up the slope that will give you some cover most of the way."

"I see it, sir," Kaminski confirmed over the radio.

"Good. There's kind of an outcropping on the right hand side. We'll follow that until we get close. We should go in slow, five kilometers an hour or so. Let's try not to get ahead of each other so we break out into the open at about the same time."

Both Elena and Kaminski gave their assent.

"I want you both to have your helmets on. We've seen what that peashooter they've got can do."

"What about you, sir?" Elena asked. She'd noticed that he hadn't included himself in the command about the helmets.

"I'm going to be riding shotgun on the outside of the buggy. If they do take a shot at us I want to be able to shoot back."

"Is that a good idea, sir?"

"Probably not, but it's the only one I've got," McKernan conceded.

"I could ride outside," Elena protested.

"It's my decision, constable. Besides, I'm probably a better shot than you are, particularly in a surface suit."

Neither of the constables contradicted the inspector.

"Any other questions?" There weren't any. "Good. Give me five minutes or so to get outside. I'll give the signal to Elena to get started, and she can relay it on to you Kaminski."

They spent the next couple of minutes getting into their suits and performing the checkout procedure. McKernan took his carbine out of its case and verified that the action was working. Then he entered the airlock.

From the driver's seat, Elena could see when the readout showed that the outer door of the airlock had opened. A moment later, she saw the inspector walking around to the front of the buggy. He waved and she waved back.

To avoid the necessity of having to cycle through the airlock every time a buggy moved, most were equipped with a jump seat that unfolded from the front. It wasn't a particularly comfortable affair, but it did save time in the field. McKernan lowered the seat and climbed up into it, fastening the seat belt. It gave him a vantage point a couple meters above the ground. He got himself comfortable with the carbine carried across his lap and then slapped his hand against the buggy to signal Elena to start moving.

As they drove forward, Elena kept her eyes on the ridgeline in front of them. She could see that McKernan was doing the same. She was worried about his exposed perch on the front of the buggy, though she had only to glance at the patched hole in the viewport to reminder her that she was really just as vulnerable. Off to her left she could see Kaminski in the other buggy, his progress paralleling their own.

When they reached the top of the ridge, the inspector signaled Elena to stop. She took the opportunity to use the binoculars to examine the area in front of them. There wasn't much to see. The surface had been completely chewed up by repeated buggy tracks, but there were no signs of any sort of building or other structure. Elena wondered if she had been mistaken about this being the location of the drug manufacturing operation.

Suddenly she caught a flash out of the corner of her eye. There was a spurt of dust a meter to the side of the buggy, and then came the faint sound of a report from a rifle. She could see McKernan raise the carbine to his shoulder and let off a burst in the direction of the flash.

Without thinking, she put the buggy in reverse and backed down the hill until they were below the ridgeline. Kaminski must have seen her, because he had backed up as well.

"I think we've found them," McKernan's dry voice came over the radio.

"Are you OK?" Kaminski asked excitedly.

"They missed," the inspector replied. "I think we'd better approach on foot from here on. It will be easier for us to cover each other."

While he waited for Ortiz to cycle through the airlock, McKernan unbuckled himself and edged to the ridgeline so that he could just peer over it. There weren't any signs of movement. Whoever had taken the shot at them had gone to ground.

When the constable came up to join him, McKernan noted that she was cradling her riot gun rather than a carbine.

"Can you see him?" Elena asked.

"No, but I think I know where he's hiding. Do you see that shadowy spot on the hillside?"

Elena looked in the direction the inspector was pointing. There was what looked to be a depression where the sun was casting a shadow. It almost looked like a cave entrance.

"What do you think it is?"

"I'm guessing it's the mouth of a lava tube. That would make sense; we're on the slope of a volcano."

Lava tubes formed when the outside of a lava flow solidified. This provided insulation for the lava in the center so it could keep flowing. When the source of the lava stopped supplying fresh lava, the still molten lava would flow out leaving behind a hollow tube. It was a type of terrain common on volcanic islands like those in Hawaii. Ortiz knew that before man had landed on Mars there had been discussion of using the tubes as bases, but as far as she was aware, no one had ever done so.

"So you think that's where they're holed up, Sir?"

"It seems logical. They wouldn't have needed to do much to turn it into a base. Put up a wall at the mouth, maybe patch a few cracks and you've got a big space you can pressurize. There wouldn't be anything showing on the surface. Sounds perfect to me."

"So how far back do you think the tunnel goes?"

"Maybe kilometers."

Kaminski, who had been listening in on the radio, asked, "So what do we do about it, sir?"

"I want you and Ortiz to work around to the sides of the entrance. Keep to cover as much as you can. I'll provide covering fire from here. When you get into position, you can cover me as I come down. I'm pretty sure the gunman is hiding in the mouth of that tube, but keep an eye open. We don't know if the tube has other entrances."

It took about fifteen minutes for the two constables to work around and get in position. Ortiz had found herself a nice boulder about thirty meters to the right of the entrance; Kaminski had taken shelter behind a low rill fifty meters away on the other side.

"OK. I'm coming down now," McKernan's voice came over the radio. "I'll be headed for that outcrop just in front of the opening. Ortiz, if you see anyone pop their heads up, let loose a blast from your shotgun."

"I'm not sure I can hit anything from this far away," Elena protested.

"You just have to make them duck. I'm coming down now."

Elena looked up and saw the inspector sprinting down the face of the ridge, or sprinting as fast as one could in a surface suit. She looked back at the opening of the lava tube. The mouth was in deep shadow, but she thought she saw something sticking out that might be the barrel of a gun. She stepped out from behind her boulder and let off a blast from the shotgun. Instinctively, she pumped the weapon to put another shell in the chamber. As she did so, she saw Kaminski raise his carbine and let off a quick burst.

When she looked back at the inspector she saw that he had taken cover behind the outcrop. She was relieved when she saw him wave his hand to show that he was alright.

"He's inside the tube," Elena called out over the radio.

McKernan had his carbine trained on the entrance. He signaled Kaminski to circle up the slope behind the opening. Elena held her shotgun ready to cover him.

Kaminski, when he got to the side of the tube, paused for a minute, and then edged across the mouth of the opening, his carbine poised to fire.

"There's only one man. He's been hit," Kaminski called into his radio.

Elena hurried to join him. What she saw when she got to the entrance was a man leaning back against the wall of the tube. He was clutching his left arm with his right hand. Through the faceplate of his suit, she could see the look of panic on his face.

CHAPTER 28

As McKernan came up to the entrance of the cave, he saw that Ortiz was trying to put an emergency patch on the surface suit of the wounded man.

"How bad is it?"

"I can't really tell. The suit was punctured by four or five pellets. I can patch the suit well enough, but I can't tell how badly he's hurt. There was some blood, but until we can get his suit off him, I can't tell if I struck an artery or not. We need to get him inside, sir."

McKernan looked around him. It looked like his guess about the hideout being a lava tube had been right. The space he was in was about ten meters wide and six meters tall in the middle. Some twenty meters into the tube a wall had been built using fused silica blocks. He couldn't tell much more, because of the lack of lighting and the two buggies that had been parked inside the tunnel.

He motioned to Kaminski to work his way down one side of the tube while he took the other. He had flipped on his helmet lights so that he could see, and as he moved towards the back wall, he looked into every nook and cranny to make sure there wasn't anyone there. He met up with Kaminski at the airlock that had been installed in the back wall. The lock looked like it had been salvaged from an old model hut, but that wasn't unusual; nothing ever went to waste on Mars. It was a larger airlock, capable of holding three or four people at once.

"Go help Ortiz move the wounded man. I'm assuming there's air pressure on the other side of this wall, and that she'll be able to look at his wounds once we get him inside."

"You going in alone, sir?"

"Someone has to. Don't come on through until I give the all clear."

McKernan pressed the control that opened the outer door of the lock. After he had entered, he checked the tell-tale for the other door. It showed that there was atmosphere on the other side. He closed the outer door and cycled the lock. When the indicator showed green, he undogged the inner door and swung it open with his foot.

"Don't shoot. I give up." The voice sounded shaken.

McKernan stepped through the hatch, his carbine up and level. Standing in front of him was a man in a surface suit, but without a helmet. From the file photo he recognized him as Jose Martin.

"Put your hands behind your head," the inspector ordered, his carbine pointed at Martin's chest. Martin did as he'd been told. "Where's Jeremy Stanton?"

"He's back there," the prisoner said, glancing back deeper into the tube.

"Ortiz, you can bring him through," McKernan said into his radio, before closing the inner hatch of the airlock.

"OK, sir. Coming through."

While McKernan waited for the lock to cycle, he looked around. This end of the tunnel had evidently been used for living quarters and storage. There were a couple of pairs of bunks, a food cooker and microwave, and shelves with cartons of supplies. A little farther back was what looked like a fairly complete machine shop. He couldn't see much farther back because of the darkness.

When the airlock hatch opened, Ortiz and Kaminski came through, supporting the wounded man between them. They laid him down on one of the bunks.

Ortiz removed his helmet and then took off her own so that she could see better. McKernan saw that it was Jackson. With Kaminski's help she slid the injured arm free of the surface suit. Martin looked a little pale as he looked on.

"It doesn't seem too bad, sir." Ortiz reported. "He needs to see a doctor, but I don't think he'll bleed to death."

"Patch him up as best you can, Elena."

"What do we do with this one?" Kaminski asked.

"Cuff him to something that isn't going to move," McKernan replied.

Kaminski prodded Martin over to a heavy table and then handcuffed the prisoner to one of the legs.

"What about the other one?" Kaminski asked.

"Martin says that he's back there somewhere." The inspector pointed back into the darkness. "Is there any way to turn on the lights?"

Martin answered meekly, "There's a switch on that breaker box that activates the overheads."

McKernan went over to the box and inspected it. A thick conduit led up from the box to the ceiling and then ran towards the depths of the tunnel. There was the arm of a switch coming out of the side of the box. The inspector threw it.

This produced a long, low whistle from Kaminski. "Some setup, sir."

McKernan had to agree. From where he stood, he could see a long row of lights on the ceiling of the lava tube extending off into the distance. Troughs had been gouged into the floor of the tube and filled with soil. Plants that McKernan didn't recognize were growing in the soil, and standing above them were piping to provide irrigation and grow lights.

"How far back does this go?" McKernan asked.

"We put another wall up about four kilometers in, but the plants only go back for a kilometer or so. We wanted to have room to expand," Martin explained sheepishly.

McKernan did the math. If the plants went back for a kilometer and the growing troughs took up two meters on each side of a central path that meant that there was roughly four thousand square meters of growing area. He didn't want to think about how many doses of the Way Back drug that would mean.

"I don't get it. Where are they getting all the power from?" Kaminski asked. "I didn't see any solar arrays on the surface."

"That was the clever part," Martin responded. "The volcano that made this lava tube isn't completely dormant. Deep down there is still a hot spot. We tapped into it to run a geothermal generator. It gave us all the power we needed."

"We can worry about that later," McKernan interrupted. "Right now we have to find Stanton."

"Like I told you, he headed towards the other end of the tube," Martin said.

"Is there another airlock back there?"

"It doesn't matter. He wasn't wearing a surface suit."

"That's something, at least," McKernan said. "Is he armed?"

"He's got a cross-bow sort of thing," Martin replied sullenly.

"That's just great. I guess we'll have to do this the hard way. Ortiz, you stay here with the prisoners. Keep that shotgun of yours handy. Kaminski, you come with me. I'll take the left side of the tunnel, you take the right. We'll work our way down the length until we find him or we reach the end."

The two lawmen started walking further back into the lava tube. The floor of the tube had been leveled out so that there was a narrow walkway on either side with a larger central path wide enough to accommodate a small vehicle. Between the path and the walkways were the plant beds along with the grow lights and drip irrigation equipment. The racks holding the lights were at the inspector's eye-level, just high enough to provide concealment for a crouching man, forcing them to advance slowly.

Every twenty meters there was a break in the growing troughs providing cross access. At each junction, there were controls for the lighting and irrigation so that each trough could be controlled individually. McKernan had to admit that the whole arrangement had been laid out in a very professional manner. He wondered what would happen to the complex. It would be a shame to let it decay when it could be used to grow food. That wasn't his problem, though, and he had more immediate concerns. Because of the necessity of checking to make sure that Stanton wasn't hiding behind the racks, it took them over twenty minutes to reach the end of the ranks of plants. They hadn't found Stanton, and, according to Martin, ahead of them stretched another three kilometers of the lava tube.

They'd also reached the end of the overhead lights. Evidently, the four drug producers hadn't gotten around to extending their improvements to the rest of the tunnel, though there were stacks of equipment waiting to be installed. There was also a small, battery powered excavator.

"What now, sir?" Kaminski asked. "I don't particularly care for the idea of walking down that tunnel using only helmet lights. Particularly if this Stanton character has got some sort of crossbow."

"I agree, constable. But maybe that excavator can solve our problem. Let's see if it's charged up."

McKernan went over the excavator, climbed into the operator's seat and hit the master switch. The control panel came to life, and a quick check showed that the battery pack had almost a full charge. A flick of another switch turned on a powerful set of headlamps.

"Well, at least we won't have to go in blind," McKernan said with a smile. "I'd offer you a ride, but there's only one seat. But if you walk behind me, you should be protected from any crossbow bolts fired our way."

The inspector played with the controls for a few seconds to familiarize himself with their operation. He discovered which one operated the bucket and raised it high enough to provide an effective shield for him.

The headlamps, powerful as they were, only illuminated the tunnel for the fifty meters directly in front of the excavator. The lava tube, however, didn't provide much in the way of cover, and McKernan didn't think that Stanton would be able to slip past them.

He kept his pace to a slow walk to make it easy for Kaminski to follow in his wake. A crude path had been plowed down the center of the tube, which made it easy enough to drive the excavator, though McKernan found that he had to give most of his attention to steering the vehicle.

It was Kaminski who spotted Stanton. They had gone nearly another kilometer, and the lights from the front of the tunnel were just a small spot behind them. Stanton had propped himself up against the side of the tunnel and was sitting there motionless.

McKernan turned the excavator so that the headlamps were centered on Stanton. The latter gave no sign that he had noticed their presence. Lying next to him was a homemade crossbow.

McKernan got off the excavator, and with Kaminski covering Stanton with his carbine, he approached him. The inspector reached out his hand and touched his shoulder but there was no reaction. When he looked at his eyes, McKernan could see they were reacting, but whatever they saw, it wasn't the inside of a lava tube on Mars.

"Is he dead?" Kaminski asked.

"No," Mckernan replied. He pried a small bottle for the sitting man's right hand. "He's taken some of his own medicine."

"How much did he take?"

Mckernan turned the bottle mouth downwards. Nothing came out.

"I don't know how many capsules were in this, but he's taken all of them."

CHAPTER 29

Elena waited nervously for the inspector and Kaminski to return. It wasn't that she was afraid. She had given Jackson a sedative along with a pain killer when she had tended his wound, and he had slipped into a semiconscious state. As for Martin, the fight had gone out of him. He had slumped down and was trying to make himself as comfortable as he could with his arm shackled to a table leg. It was just that the waiting was getting to her, and staring down the length of the tunnel wasn't helping any.

She was relieved when she finally saw the excavator driving toward her driven by McKernan with Kaminski walking next to it. As it got closer she noticed the body cradled in the excavator's bucket. She hadn't heard any sounds of gunfire, but Stanton, and by elimination the body had to be Stanton's, was clearly more of a casualty than a prisoner.

The inspector pulled up and lowered the bucket gently to the ground before turning the excavator off.

"Do I need the first-aid kit?" Elena asked.

"I don't think there's much you can do for him. Stanton is off in his own private memory world. Rather than face us, it looks like he took some of his own Memory Dust, a lot of it. I'm not sure if he's ever coming back. How's Jackson?"

"I've patched him up as best as I can. He's not bleeding that I can see. I've given him something for the pain and a sedative to keep him quiet."

"Did the other one give you any trouble?"

"No, he's been quiet since you left."

McKernan went over to the prisoner. Martin looked up at him in defeat.

"Any idea how much Way Back Stanton had on him?"

"Way Back? Oh, you mean Memory Dust. He always kept a dozen capsules on him. He said he'd take the whole batch rather than be captured. We all thought he was just being dramatic, but I guess he really meant it. He actually went ahead and did it, didn't he?"

"Yeah," McKernan said disgustedly.

"What's going to happen to us?" Martin asked.

"I'll take you back to Mars City. I imagine you'll be put on the first available rocket to Earth. What happens after that is out of my hands. You may get some prison time, or maybe nothing at all will happen. I'm not sure that you've broken any actual laws, though a couple of men are dead because of you."

"You know that we didn't kill Ian, don't you?"

"I didn't say you had," McKernan replied, suddenly feeling tired. "Why don't you tell me what happened."

"It had started to get to him, living here in the back of the Out There. He was getting a little squirrelly. I think he just wanted to go back to Earth. One day when the rest of us were sleeping, he snuck out and took one of the buggies. Freddy and I went after him, but he had too much of a head start. I guess when he got to the road he must have taken some dust and forgotten where he was."

Mckernan looked at Martin who seemed to be feeling genuine remorse for what had happened.

"So why didn't you just leave him there?"

"When we finally found him, it was obvious that someone had been there first. I guess we kind of panicked.

We were afraid of being discovered. We put him on one of the buggies and then drove back here."

"Stopping on the way to bury your friend in the middle of nowhere," McKernan commented.

"Well, he was dead. There wasn't anything we could do about that. Freddy and I found a place and buried the body. We didn't just leave him," Martin protested. "We put up a marker."

"You stuck a rod in the sand," McKernan corrected harshly. "What about his family? Did you think about that?"

"Ian didn't really have any family to speak of. That's one of the reasons he decided to come to Mars in the first place. We did the best we could under the circumstances. Jeremy was getting a little squirrelly, too, but in a different way. What does it matter, anyhow? Ian was dead. If we had left him, he'd just have been put in another hole in the sand someplace else and forgotten about."

McKernan looked as though he was about to say something and then just shook his head. "Maybe you're right. Maybe it doesn't make any difference."

Elena could see that the inspector was tired. They all were.

"What do we do now, sir?"

"I say we get out of here and head back to Junction 3. I can catch the road train from there. Stanton and Jackson can ride with you, Kaminski. Neither one of them is in any shape to give you much trouble. We'll take Martin with us."

They had quite a struggle getting Stanton into his surface suit and out into Kaminski's buggy. Stanton was unresponsive, though he would occasionally twitch his muscles spasmodically in the manner of a dreaming dog. It took the efforts of all three of them to get him into the buggy and lashed to the jump seat. Jackson was a little easier to handle, but it took the better part of an hour to get set to leave.

"What do we do with this place?" Elena asked after they had exited the tunnel airlock for the last time.

"We don't have anything to lock it up with; not that would make a difference. Slap a piece of crime scene tape across the airlock and let's get out of here. We'll drive until dark, and stop for the night."

They had driven nearly a hundred kilometers south before they stopped. They still had hours of driving to do the next day and Elena knew they wouldn't get to Junction 3 until late in the day. She found herself missing Mike and Miguel.

Once they had stopped, Elena pulled three meal packs out of the storage locker, handed one to Martin who was cuffed in the jump seat, and took the other two up to the front seats.

"Pasta and meatballs or chicken gumbo, sir?"

"Either one's fine with me. What did you give the prisoner?"

"Beans and rice. And water."

McKernan smiled. Elena handed the inspector one of meal packs.

"Any more of that joy juice? I could use a drink."

Elena went to the back of the buggy and returned with the bottle, handing it to McKernan. He took it, poured some in his cup and passed it back to her.

Neither one said much during dinner. Martin ate his in silence. It was only when they were done that he spoke up.

"You know we never meant to hurt anyone."

"Look how well that turned out. I should remind you that anything you say can and will be used as evidence against you."

"Does it matter?" Martin responded.

"Probably not. Constable, turn on the recorder."

Elena reached over and pressed a button on the console and said, "Statement of Jose Martin, Chief Inspector McKernan and Constable Ortiz present."

"So why did you do it?" McKernan asked.

"We all knew each other in college. Coming to Mars seemed like a good idea. You both know how opportunities are limited on Earth, or you wouldn't be here. We thought we'd come to Mars and make our fortunes. We did alright, but our three year contracts were ending and none of us was rich. But Jeremy had this plan. His uncle had left him some seeds and information on the process for turning the plants into the drug he called Memory Dust. No one knew that he had the seeds or that they even existed. He kept trying to talk us into going in with him. Well, we didn't really have any better options. It was either sign up for another three years or go back to Earth. We started to take him seriously as it got closer to the time our contracts were up.

"The way Jeremy described it, the drug just lets you get away for a few hours to some happier time in your past. And that's what it does. It sounds harmless enough, and for most people it is. But if the present isn't working out so good for you, or the stresses are getting too great—well, the temptation is just to keep taking it more often or to take more of it at a time. I guess we didn't realize that at the time, not even Jeremy, I don't think. We just thought of it as a way to make some easy money.

"Anyway, we formed this plan. The four of us would go in together, pool the money we had when our contracts expired. We all had useful skills. I knew about the lava tube, Freddy is a genius mechanically, Jeremy knew all about growing plants, and Ian—well Ian knew what chemical engineering we needed to transform the plants into the Memory Dust.

"We went into it, and at first it was fun, all just a big adventure. We got the tube set up and started raising the plants. Ian made the first batch. He took it in to Hut Town. After word of mouth got around, we didn't have much trouble selling it, either. Plenty of guys were willing to pay a few dollars or whatever to take a few hour mental vacation. We thought we had it made."

There was a pause in the narrative. For a moment Elena thought Martin had decided that he had said enough, but then he continued.

"But then a few guys started overdoing it. Taking it too often or taking too much. Of course, we didn't hear about that at first because no one was sure what was happening. But by that time we were in it too deep. We'd sunk all our money into equipping the tube. If we had stopped we would have ended up with nothing. Maybe we should have. I'm pretty sure Ian was thinking about it. But Jeremy wouldn't let us. He kept urging us on. Said it wasn't our fault if people ended up abusing the dust. He said that we'd been up front about the potential side effects, which we had. Or at least, I always was. But we'd gotten into it, and then we couldn't see any way out."

"What about the crossbows and the gun?" McKernan asked.

"I guess we all got a little paranoid. We were making money, and you know that there are some unscrupulous people on Mars—"

McKernan didn't bother to point out the irony.

"What about shooting at Constable Ortiz?"

"That was Jeremy. When we told him that someone had found Ian's body before Freddy and I, he got worried about someone following us and decided to wait in ambush. He said he was just trying to scare them off."

"He came damn near to killing the constable," McKernan stated angrily.

"Jeremy always did take things too far."

"Jackson took a shot at me, as well," McKernan pointed out.

"I guess we panicked."

McKernan didn't say anything in response.

"Like I said, we never wanted for anyone to get hurt. Things just got out of hand."

"I guess they did," the inspector commented after a moment. "You know what the funny thing is?"

"I don't understand."

"If the four of you had decided to grow vegetables or fruit in that cave of yours, you could have become rich. Hell, even if you didn't want to farm, you could have gone into the business of setting up lava tubes for agriculture and selling them."

"I guess we didn't think about that," Martin admitted sadly.

McKernan shook his head. "Is there anything more you want to add?"

"No, I guess not."

"I suggest we all get some sleep then."

CHAPTER 30

McKernan took the road train back to Mars City. With three prisoners and a body to accompany him, arranging for a plane had seemed impractical. Besides, the day and a half it would take to get to Mars City would give him time to unwind and write his report. He knew that with the election coming up on Friday, once he got home, he would be kept busy until after the voting was completed.

With people traveling to the city to be in the center of things during the big event, the train was more crowded than usual to the point that an extra trailer had been added to accommodate the additional passengers. McKernan had arranged seats for his three charges in the baggage wagon where his prisoners could be isolated from the rest of the passengers. Jackson had recovered to the point where he could be shackled to his seat as was Martin. As Stanton was still unresponsive, it didn't seem to matter whether he was cuffed or not.

Being in range of the cell towers along the road, the inspector was able to check up on the preparations for the election. As far as he could tell, all the people responsible were as ready as they could be.

McKernan was glad when the road train finally reached Mars City after nearly thirty-six hours straight traveling with only brief stops at Junction Two and One. He turned the prisoners over to Gaeretts and headed home.

Beth had managed to get her hands on a pair of beef sirloin steaks imported from Earth. There was a nice wine, as well, even if it had come from a pouch rather than a bottle, though he noticed Beth didn't drink much of it. He thought that there was something on her mind, but he was too tired to inquire. Shortly after dinner was done the inspector fell asleep on the couch. Beth had to wake him to get him into the bedroom.

There was an e-mail invitation from Otis McAndrews waiting for him in the morning. While not exactly a command, McAndrews, as the local head of Anglo-Martian and the longest residing leader of any of the mining companies, was the unofficial spokesman for the corporations and not someone he could refuse. But it wasn't only for that reason that McKernan accepted the invitation. McAndrews had for some time been both a friend and mentor to the inspector. McKernan also knew that he kept a supply of excellent single malt Scotch on hand.

McAndrews had recently moved from an apartment in the Anglo-Martian office block to a residence in Mars City's latest addition, Syrtis Gardens. What with the preparations for the election and his other problems, McKernan hadn't had a chance to inspect the new luxury residential block since it had been completed, and he was curious to see how it had turned out.

The invitation had been for 2000, and after dinner, McKernan started the long walk from Hut Town. Like almost all of the new construction, the residential block was on the south side of Mars City, the side opposite from Hut Town. He realized he had quite a walk ahead of him. If the city kept expanding, sooner or later some form of public transit would have to be put in place.

Passing through the Concourse, he noted that things were quiet, though there seemed to be more people milling around than usual. If nothing else, one positive thing to come out of the election was that people seemed to be interacting with others beyond those they worked with. Erik smiled. Mars was starting to become a community.

When he finally reached the end of the corridor leading to Syrtis Gardens, McKernan found himself facing the inevitable air-tight door. As with most of the similar doors in Mars City proper, this one was kept open, but it was ready to close instantly at any sign of a drop in air pressure. When he stepped over the lip of the opening, McKernan found himself in another world.

The rest of Mars City was uniformly utilitarian, consisting of walls of fused silica bricks, floors of fused silica tiles and ceilings of thin plastic panels designed to be easily removable to provide access to whatever infrastructure was hidden behind them. The color scheme was a bland mixture of white and beige. What Erik now found himself in was a two story atrium, whose ten meters of height was capped by a skylight. Looking up, he felt a moment of panic. As a long time Martian, he wasn't comfortable with the idea of there being nothing solid between him and the almost nonexistent atmosphere of Mars. A closer inspection revealed that the skylight consisted of at least three layers of glass, each one presumably air-tight.

Reassured, he lowered his gaze to look around him. What he saw mostly, was green. A row of planters flanked either side of the atrium, so thick with shrubbery and plants that they almost concealed the walls from view. Several small trees had been strategically placed along the center line of the atrium. There were even two small pools located at each end, and when McKernan passed the one nearest him, he noted the flashing scales of a Koi fish. Balconies jutted out from the second floor. The railings consisted of ornate aluminum castings that had been treated to give them the patina of antique bronze. Under foot, he noticed that the paving was either actual stone, or tiles that gave a convincing illusion of that material.

All in all, it reminded McKernan of nothing so much as the French Quarter of New Orleans. Of course, it was all an artificial construct, but the illusion was effective. It must have cost a fortune to build and maintain, McKernan thought. With amusement, he noted the grow lights that were attached to the underside of the balconies. The skylights alone would never be able to admit enough light to sustain the plant life.

What struck him most, though, was the smell. It was the smell of Earth. Most of the scents of Mars were a combination of the smell of stale human bodies, the odors of cooking, burnt lubricating oil, and the ill-defined, arid smell of Martian dust which seemed to get everywhere. None of these were in evidence in Syrtis Gardens. Erik wondered how long it had been since he had last smelled Earth. He realized that it had been nearly a decade.

The address Erik had been given was "No. 5." As the atrium was only fifty meters long, it wouldn't be hard to find. The odd numbers were on his left and the even on the right. With only six units on each side, No. 5 was in the middle on the left. He made his way around a large potted fern to the door marked five. As with all construction on Mars, the door was air-tight, but it had been given a skin of simulated wood planking. He pushed the button next to the door and waited.

It only took a moment for the door to open, and he was greeted by a short, Hispanic looking man.

"Chief Inspector. Please come in. Mr. McAndrews is expecting you." The servant's appearance might have been Latin, but his accent was pure Glaswegian.

McKernan found himself in a small foyer that could have been in a house anywhere on Earth. The floor was made of the same stone as that used in the atrium, except that it had been covered with a rug in pale blue. The walls met at right angles to the floor and had been painted a light green. There was even wood trim, or something that looked very much like it.

"Mr. McAndrews is upstairs in his study," his greeter said, indicating a circular staircase with his hand.

He climbed the stairs to a pleasant room that ran the width of the unit facing the atrium. A glass door gave out onto the small balcony. Only careful inspection revealed the air-tight seal around its rim. Two bookcases filled with print books were against either side wall, along with several landscapes which Erik assumed were of Scotland. All that was missing to complete the scene was a fireplace, but, then, that would have been taking things too far.

The furnishings looked comfortable, though it was obvious that they had been designed to be knocked down flat and assembled on site. The cushions were thin, but with the lower gravity of Mars, that wasn't a problem. The colors were muted with the exposed wood natural. The effect was vaguely Scandinavian from the previous century.

McAndrews had stood to greet him, and Erik gladly took the offered hand.

"I'm glad you could make it, Erik. Please have a seat. Manuel should be up in a moment with something from Speyside."

Erik sat in a chair while McAndrews took one near it facing him at an angle. True to his word, Manuel appeared bearing a tray with a bottle, two glasses, and a small carafe of water.

"Will there be anything else, Mr. McAndrews?"

"Thank you, no, Manuel. I think we are set for the moment."

Manuel made a hint of a bow and turned to descend the staircase.

"I don't know what I would do without Manuel. This place would be quite lonely without him. Too bad he'll be going back to Earth in another year. Oh, well. I suppose the company will send someone else to replace him."

From that, Erik assumed that the butler was on Mars on a standard three year contract. That was typical. Most people came to Mars with the intention of making a lot of money while having nothing much to spend it on, and then returning to Earth. Quite a few of them did, but not all, he reflected.

McAndrews went through the ritual of opening the bottle of Scotch, pouring several fingers worth in each of the two glasses and adding a splash of water. Erik didn't recognize the label, but he had no doubt that it was top-notch. When he was handed one of the glasses he could almost smell the heather, peat, and a hint of salt-spray.

"To Mars."

After the toast, Erik cradled his glass in his hand as he waited for McAndrews to open the conversation. The older man, obviously aware of the other's feelings, hesitated only a moment to savor the Scotch.

"You're probably wondering why I invited you here tonight." McAndrews smiled at his own cliché.

"The thought had occurred to me," Erik responded dryly.

"Let's just say that I've become aware of some unease on your part about the future." McAndrews, when serious, had a tendency to lapse into more formal phrasings. "If I can, I'd like to alleviate that unease."

"I appreciate that, sir, though I'm not sure—"

McAndrews interrupted.

"Before you respond, why don't you tell me what you see for yourself in the coming years?"

"That's just it, I guess. With some sort of home rule starting to look like a reality, I'm not sure what exactly the future holds for me. As a member of the Security Force, I'm an employee of the Trust Authority. I'm not even sure that there *will* be a Security Force once a local government is established."

"I don't think you need to have any worries on that account, Erik. Any new government will need some sort of law enforcement agency, and I'm sure that there will be a place in it for you. You've made a lot of friends over the years—"

"And a lot of enemies," Erik countered.

McAndrews smiled. "But most of your real enemies are no longer around." The implication was that they had either been returned to Earth—or were dead. "It's your friends that matter. You've earned the respect and trust of most of us on Mars. I think both the Red and the Green parties would be happy to see you continue on in your current role. And as for the companies, well, I think I can speak for them, and we've always been more than satisfied with the way you've carried out your duties. Whatever the future security arrangements are, I think people would be comfortable with you in charge."

"I'm glad to hear that, sir."

"You understand that I can't officially give you any guarantees, but I can assure you of the companies' full support."

Erik wasn't quite sure how to respond, so he took another sip of the whisky in his hand.

McAndrews allowed a moment of silence. Erik, as he studied the face of his friend, thought he looked relieved at having gotten the purpose of the meeting out of the way. He took a sip from his own glass and then asked, "Tell me, Erik, have you ever thought about going back to Earth?"

"I don't think there's anything left for me back there. I'm not sure there ever was. I don't have any close family, and I'm not sure what I would do with myself if I were to go back. As they say, if you sign up for the second three years, you're never going to go back."

"Spoken like a true Martian," McAndrews commented. "I'm in much the same boat, Erik, though in my case it is my body that has exiled me to Mars. I don't think I would live long if I were to return."

"I hope you're in good health, sir."

"Oh, Dr. Greenwood assures me that I'm as sound as can be expected at my age. As long as I remain in the lower gravity of Mars, that is."

"I'm glad to hear that."

"Oh, I have no regrets, Erik. I've lived a full life. As you know, I've had my adventures, maybe more than I would have liked. And I like to feel that I've been part of building something here. A new world if you will. I wonder if your American pioneers felt the same way?"

"I think some of them did. Jefferson, Franklin."

"I'd be curious to know if sometime in the future they'll be putting portraits of either of us on Martian currency," McAndrews quipped. "An appalling thought, isn't it?"

"I don't think we have to worry. They'll probably use Tokara or Peterson."

There was a lull in the conversation.

"It seems a shame to waste good whisky on such matters. Tell me, Erik, how are things with you and Dr. Haestert, these days?"

"She's well, sir."

"But is she happy?"

"Sometimes. She loves her work. She's adjusted to conditions on Mars—"

"But she hasn't committed herself to staying."

"No. Not fully." Erik took another sip before continuing, "You know that she had applied for a position on Earth."

"Yes, I had heard."

"The selfish part of me was relieved when she wasn't accepted, but I wonder sometimes if it would have been better if she had had the opportunity to go back. At least then it would have been her choice to stay or not."

"I hope it works out, Erik. For both of your sakes. Mars needs women like the doctor. And men like you, Erik."

"And like you, sir."

Erik drained his glass.

"My, haven't we gotten maudlin. I'm afraid good Scotch late at night will do that to you. By the way, I notice your glass is empty, Erik. Would you care for another?"

"It's hard to refuse good whisky, but make it a small one. I'm afraid I have a busy day ahead of me."

"The election?" McAndrews said as he refilled Erik's glass. He topped off his own as well.

"What else," Erik said with a wry smile.

Neither man seemed willing to continue that thread of conversation. For a long minute they sat in silence. Erik found himself staring at one of the landscapes on the wall. Something about it seemed wrong, but then he realized that it was too green in color.

"What do *you* think about this idea of terraforming Mars, Erik? That seems to be the big difference between the Pragmatists and the Futurists, isn't it? In most other ways they seem in complete agreement."

"I can't say that I've thought all that much about it, sir. After all, even if it could be done, Mars wouldn't show the effects in my lifetime."

"But in your children's or grandchildren's lifetimes?"

"I don't have any offspring. But one of my constables does, a real Martian, born here on Mars. I do wonder what sort of planet he will grow up on. But do we have the right to change Mars, and try to make it into something it wasn't meant to be?"

"We did it to Earth," McAndrews responded.

"And look how well that has turned out," Erik answered.

Silence followed, but the conversation lasted well into the night.

CHAPTER 31

Elena was glad when they finally pulled into Junction 3. While working on a major case with the Chief Inspector again had been professionally rewarding, she wasn't sorry that it was finished. This was the place that she had come to call home; the place where Mike and Miguel were. She had to admit, too, that she was looking forward to being able to change out of her surface suit and the prospect of food that didn't come out of a meal pack.

She noted that, though it was only Tuesday and Election Day wasn't until Friday, there were already an unusually large number of buggies standing in the empty space that served as a parking lot for the hotel. People must be coming early to secure the limited number of accommodations. Late arrivals would probably end up having to sleep in their buggies.

She helped McKernan secure the prisoners. The security office didn't have an actual cell, just a room with a stout door and a lock, but neither Martin nor Jackson looked as though they posed much of a flight risk. As for Stanton, he was still lost in his private world of memories. In any case, the prisoners wouldn't be there long; the land train was due at Junction 3 that afternoon, and McKernan would escort them along with the body all the way to Mars City.

Kaminski was going to spend the night at Junction 3, taking the opportunity for a hot shower and one of Jenny's home cooked meals before driving the thousand kilometers back to his base at Junction 5. He was responsible for monitoring Election Day there, but that promised to be a much more sparsely attended event than it was shaping up to be at Junction 3.

McKernan had told her that he and Kaminski would see to putting the prisoners on the train when it arrived and that she should go home to Mike and Miguel. She hadn't refused.

Elena was up bright and early on Election Day, crossing over the road to have breakfast at the hotel. It appeared that other people had had the same idea; the dining room was full to capacity and the crowd was spilling over into any space where they could find room. The population of Junction 3, which normally numbered around a hundred permanent residents, had swelled to over five hundred and the place was literally bursting at the seams.

Jenny had reserved a table for the election officials, so they wouldn't have to wait, and Elena took a place alongside the three people she had appointed to oversee the balloting. One of these was Jenny's husband, the other two ran local businesses. With so many people to feed, the menu was limited to fried potatoes with peppers, onions, and a little bacon, but Jenny had managed to add a fried egg to each of the election official's plates. Coffee was in short supply, there just weren't enough pots to brew it in to keep everyone's cups filled.

By 0745 they had finished their breakfast. Balloting began promptly at 0800. The procedure was simple enough. People would grab a ballot. Once they had marked it, selecting up to three names from the list of potential delegates, they would bring it to the official's table which had been set up in the hotel lobby. At the table their name would be entered as having voted and their ballot would be handed to Jenny's husband who would place it in the ballot box in full view of everyone. The voter's hand would then be stamped so they couldn't vote a second time, but as everyone knew everyone else, there was little chance of that happening.

The voting was orderly, though the line quickly snaked out of sight. There was a lot of discussion amongst those in line, but everyone seemed to be in a good mood.

By noon, it appeared that everyone present had voted. Elena went through the building calling out to make sure that there wasn't anyone left before making the announcement that they all had been waiting for:

"The polling is now closed. The bar is open."

This last announcement produced a cheer that shook the building.

The election officials retired to the security office and began the process of tabulating the ballots. Each party had put up a slate of a dozen candidates, and there had been seven people running as independents. The top twelve vote getters Mars wide would be named as delegates to the convention that would determine the principles which would serve as the basis for negotiating home rule. They would also be responsible for selecting the members of the committee that would travel to Earth to carry out the negotiations with the U.N.

Elena wasn't surprised that when the votes were tallied; five Red and five Green delegates along with two independents had come out ahead in the balloting, with a slight edge in the total number of votes going to the Red party. Sentiments had been running fairly even in recent weeks, and the truth was there wasn't that much difference in the platforms of either party. She wasn't surprised, though, that the two top vote getters at Junction 3 had been local residents.

After securing the signatures of each of the officials validating the results, Elena placed a call to the election headquarters in Mars City. Then she went out to announce the results to the waiting crowd and join the party.

Chapter 32

It was in that time peculiar to Mars, the forty odd minutes between midnight and the start of a new day occasioned by the slightly longer Martian rotational period, that, McKernan finally made his way home to Hut Town. As he made his way down the corridor, he met a few groups of people still out celebrating. They seemed to be in a uniformly good mood, though how much of that was due to the election results and how much were the effects of alcohol was anyone's guess.

All in all, the election had gone off well. The lines had been long at first, everyone seeming to have decided to get their vote in early, but people had for the most part been patient and courteous. There had been a few cases where people had complained that they wanted to vote when they weren't eligible under the rules that had been established. In most of those cases, McKernan had allowed the vote to be cast on the theory that anyone who wanted to vote that badly should have the chance. As far as he knew, there had been no cases of voter fraud anywhere on Mars.

Between Mars City and Hut Town, over eighteen thousand ballots had been cast. The outlying stations and mining operations had contributed another twelve thousand. Surprisingly, less than two thousand votes had been cast electronically. It seemed that most people had wanted to experience the historic occasion in the presence of their fellow Martians.

The results, when they had finally been tabulated, had been close, with the Pragmatists taking a slight lead in total votes. It looked as though many people had voted for the person rather than a party, because the delegates selected had been split evenly with five for each party along with two independents, both of whom were well known and well respected long time residents.

Peterson had gotten the most votes, Tokara had come in second. The current Trust Authority Governor had announced the final results to a packed Concourse just after 2300. Live video of the event had been beamed all over Mars, and a couple of large monitors set up on the Concourse had displayed video feeds from Junction 3 and several of the larger mining camps. When Peterson had been invited up to make a speech, he had called Tokara up to the stage and shaken his hand. The two then pledged to work together for the betterment of Mars. There had been a lot of back slapping and handshaking in the crowd along with a fair amount of hugging and kissing.

It had taken nearly fifteen minutes before the crowd had quieted down enough for Peterson to give his speech. It was brief and drew a long round of applause. Tokara spoke at more length, but the applause was as loud. After that the crowd had started to thin, and McKernan had felt that the situation was such that he could leave it in Gaeretts's and Ferris's hands and head home.

Beth was waiting up for him when he came through the airlock. She had said that she was too tired to attend the announcement on the Concourse.

"Sorry it's so late," McKernan apologized. "It took longer than expected to get the results in from some of the outposts."

"That's okay, Erik. I understand. Would you like a drink?"

"I could use one. It's been a long day."

Beth poured him a glass from a bottle of Scotch that McAndrews had given them for Christmas. He noticed that she didn't make a drink for herself. She'd been doing that a lot lately, and Erik wondered if it meant anything more than that she was tired and had to be at the hospital in the morning. He took the drink and sat down on the couch, glad to finally get off his feet. Even with the low gravity of Mars, it had been a long day. Beth sat next to him, leaning in. He put his arm around her, and she pressed closer.

"I watched the announcement on video. Everything seemed to go well."

"It worked out about as well as one could hope for. As far as I can tell almost everyone was happy with the results."

"What do you think is going to happen now?"

"Nothing much, at least in the short term. No matter what they decide in the end, it's going to take the U.N. a long time to make up their minds. Probably years. But I think it's inevitable that Mars will be getting more control over its own affairs."

"And how will that affect us, Erik?" Beth said, suddenly sounding very serious.

"I had a long talk with Otis last night. He went out of his way to assure me that I had the backing of the companies and that I didn't have to worry about my job. As for you, Mars needs doctors. You've got a place at the hospital as long as you want it. You know that, don't you?"

"Erik, there's something I need to tell you."

McKernan felt a moment of panic. Was Beth finally going to tell him that she was returning to Earth?

"What is it, Beth?"

There was a moment of silence as if she was dreading what she had to say next.

"I'm pregnant, Erik. We're going to have a child. A Martian child. I hope I'm ready for that."

"You will be, Beth. We will be."

SPECIAL PREVIEW!

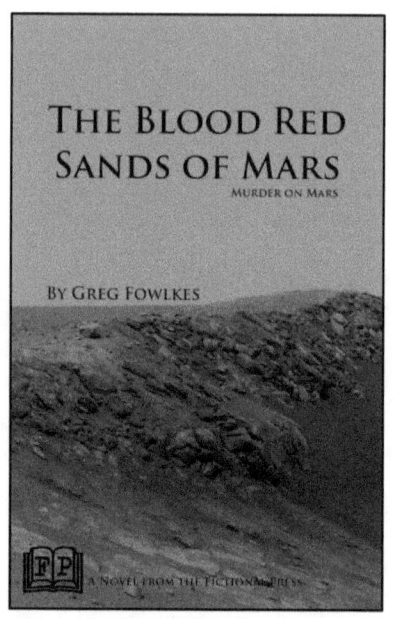

THE BLOOD RED
SANDS OF MARS
By Greg Fowlkes

Book One from the Murder on Mars Series

Now available from The Fictional Press
www.TheFictionalPress.com

THE BLOOD RED SANDS OF MARS

The wind was blowing again against the west wall of the hut. He could hear the grains of sand abrading the thin aluminum skin that protected him from the outside. Through the window, half frosted from the continuous onslaught of sand and dust, he could see clouds of dust obscuring the sky. The sky was a pastel pink, a color no sky had any right to be. The wind, despite its 120 kph. velocity, made only a thin howl as it blew over the half buried cylinder of the hut.

McKernan lay on his cot trying not to admit that he was awake. It was a losing battle. After a few minutes he surrendered and glanced over at the clock sitting on the crate next to his bed. The dim red digits of the LED display read 7:58. It was too early to get up, too late to go back to sleep. He rolled over, shivering at the cold. The temperature couldn't have been more than ten degrees Celsius inside the hut. For the twentieth time he thought to himself that he would have to fix the heater before winter—if he could get the parts. Either that, or put in more insulation—if he could find that. The cold finally forced the decision to get up.

Standing, he felt the cold plastic floor beneath his bare feet. With his foot he fished the worn and patched pants from beneath the cot and pulled them on. He dug underneath his pillow and came up with a switchblade knife that he stuck in his pocket before drawing on the turtleneck sweater that had lain next to his pants. The cold feel of the cloth did nothing to dispel the cold from his body. From the crate he picked up a shoulder holster with a small automatic pistol and put it on. McKernan drew the weapon, worked the slide once, and after examining it perfunctorily, placed it back in the holster. Satisfied, he pulled on a worn pair of leather boots and placed another knife in a sheathe between his skin and the boot top.

Dressed, he went over to the shelf that served as counter and table. He put a pan of beans onto the heating unit and got a soysteak from the small refrigerator that held up one end of the shelf. The steak went into the frying pan on the other heating element. An egg would have been nice, but at the current price of three dollars apiece it was an extravagance that he would have to put off for a while.

As the food cooked he drew a liter of water from the spigot in the corner of the hut and watered the plants in the garden under the window. The carrots and tomatoes were doing nicely. He smiled briefly because it would be good to have fresh vegetables for a change. The big, leafy oxygen plants were doing well, too. He would be able to cut down on his oxygen ration this month and save some money.

He took the beans off the heating element and replaced them with the coffee pot. The beans were still half cold, but he wasn't in the mood to hassle with them. He only had the two heating elements, and he didn't want to have to wait for his coffee. He forced down the beans and then wolfed down the steak. It almost tasted like real beef, but then maybe his memories were fading. As usual, the coffee tasted terrible and tepid, too. The air pressure in the hut was too low for water to boil properly.

He finished his meal and scraped the remnants of food into the pressure vessel that served as a compost heap. The gauge on its neighbor showed that he had almost half a tank of methane. He'd be able to sell that soon and use the money for something useful, like a still. Completing his rounds, the gauges on the life support systems showed that everything was still working at keeping him alive. He went back to the pots and scrubbed them clean with sand. That, at least, was plentiful and cheap.

He checked his watch against the clock. It was time to get going. Pulling on his jacket he went to the airlock at the corridor end of the hut. After checking the gauge to make sure that there was pressure on the other side, he undogged the latches and stepped through. Closing the door behind him, he repeated the process with the outer hatch, latching both doors behind him. The outer door he locked with a heavy padlock.

He had entered a low tubular corridor made of the same aluminum foil and plastic foam construction as the hut. The walls, however, were even thinner, and no pretense was made of heating it. He could see his breath condensing in front of him as he began to walk down its length. It was a hell of a way to live, he reflected, not for the first time. But then, it had been hell living in L.A. where he'd been born, with brown air, rats, a chronic shortage of water, and overcrowded tenements. He had made his choice, but sometimes it seemed as though life was a continual shiver.

The corridor was pierced at regular intervals by hatches identical to his own. The huts behind the hatches were identical, too, except for the modifications the owners had made to make them more livable. This part of the city was old, dating back a couple of decades to the first days of the settlement when it had been part of a scientific base. The scientists had departed, at least from that corridor, and been replaced by those who had the money to buy or rent the huts from the Trust Authority. Maintenance was pretty much left up to the residents.

Along the sides and overhead ran the pipes and conduits that pumped in the gases, liquids, and power necessary for sustaining life. The whole system looked as jury rigged and fragile as it actually was, though surprisingly few people died whenever the system failed. Martians were a cautious lot. One didn't talk much about injuries. Accidents on Mars didn't leave many.

A hundred meters down the tube he came to an airlock. Going through the same ritual that he had used on his front door, he went through to another length of corridor indistinguishable from the one he had just left. Continuing on, he passed through two more airlocks until he entered a corridor that sloped downward. The hatches were farther apart, and larger. Signs overhead indicated the businesses or functions that were carried out behind them. The air was warmer because the corridor was buried beneath the sand which provided insulation. At the end of the tunnel was a larger airlock set into a wall of fused silica bricks, the first substantial piece of construction he had met that morning.

Passing through the portal was like entering another world, which in a way he had. This was the public Mars, the planet seen by the corporation men and the officials of the Trust Authority. It was also the planet seen by tourists, the brave new colony, man's first outpost on another planet. The tourists didn't really care to see the hut town. They were part of the same world as the corporation men and the government types. It still took a great deal of money or power to reach Mars.

The difference was more than one of degree. For one thing, the temperature was a comfortable twenty. For another, the walls were flat and met the floors and ceilings at right angles, unlike the inflated skins of the huts and corridors. With a little imagination it could almost be an enclosed shopping mall on earth, though the presence of fused silica blocks was more prevalent than any architect would allow.

The most important difference, however, was the sight of people scurrying along. He hadn't met anyone in the outer corridors. People rarely lingered there because of the cold. Now, McKernan could see at least twenty people and it was still fairly early. No airlocks interrupted this corridor. Extending for two hundred meters in either direction, it was twenty meters wide and ten high, the largest enclosed volume on the planet. Arrayed along its length were the offices and store fronts of the corporations that owned Mars, as well as the more prosperous saloons and bordellos.

One day the Trust Authority promised that the whole city would be like that, with apartments and condominiums for the ordinary workers, but neither the Authority or the corporations had yet come up with the money. For the moment all that existed was the one street of a few blocks.

McKernan headed towards the Authority's offices which dominated one end of the mall, but turned aside at the last moment when he noticed that a small, dark doorway was open. He knew that he should resist the temptation, but he was not in a very disciplined mood. He went through the doorway into the darkness beyond.

Finnegan's was the only real, honest bar on Mars. There were any number of saloons and even a cocktail lounge in the Mars Sheraton, but only one quiet, dark place where a man could drink in peace. McKernan felt the need for some of that peace at the moment.

He sat down on one of the stools before the only mahogany bar on Mars. Finnegan, himself, was behind the bar, though in fact he almost always was, no matter what the hour.   The bartender looked up and greeted the newcomer, "Good morning, constable. Beer or whiskey?"

"It's too early for beer. It's too early for whiskey, but give me a shot, anyway."

Finnegan poured out a shot glass of amber liquid and placed it before McKernan and then stood back polishing a glass while he studied the man opposite him.

McKernan knocked back half the glass before he spoke. When he did, there was a bitter edge to his voice. "Sometimes I wonder if it's worth it, Finnegan. I could be back on a planet fit for human life."

"Could you, now, constable?" Finnegan said, putting down the glass and picking up another in equally gleaming condition. "If mother earth was such a bed of roses, why are you here?"

He breathed on the glass and examined it against the light for a moment, then looked at McKernan with the same intentness. "You're here because you're not the sort to live off the dole or to spend your life with another man being your boss. Instead you'll spend your life trying to make this planet a fit place to live and retire in twenty years with a nice pension. Now drink up and get to work, laddy."

"Yeah, sure. Sorry to burden you with my problems. Early morning depression, I guess. See you." He finished off the shot and left five dollars in Authority script on the bar.

———————

The bite of the whiskey so early in the morning didn't really help his disposition, but it did give him enough courage to make it to the office. The morning ritual at Finnegan's was becoming too much of a habit. His three years on Mars were beginning to show.

The jail wasn't in the brick part of the Authority building, but in the complex of pneumatic architecture that sprawled behind it. The huts were old—older than his own—but dated back to the days when governments had not begrudged a few billions for exploration, back before space had to show a profit. For that reason, they were sound and well insulated, though a bit tacky looking.

The jail consisted of two huts joined together, one for offices, the other for the two makeshift cells and storage. Ferris was the only one there when he walked in, a young kid, younger than he had been himself when he had come to Mars. He was still impressed enough with his responsibilities and had not yet been worn down by the grim realities to take his job in any way but seriously.

Ferris greeted him with a solemn, "Good morning, sir," with a stress on the sir. As a three year veteran of Mars, Ferris looked on his boss with more than a touch of awe.

"Anything exciting happen overnight?" McKernan didn't really expect much. A few fights in the saloon district, a knifing maybe if things got out of hand. Petty thievery, or perhaps not so petty. He looked at Ferris and saw a flash of excitement in his eyes that the younger man was trying hard to suppress in order to match the hard bitten image he had of his superior.

"Yes, sir. We've got a murder on our hands."

"Another knifing down at Thelma's?" he asked, naming an infamous saloon and bordello that figured in a quarter of all the police reports.

"No. A prospector was found out on his claim yesterday, over on the far side of Olympus Mons. He was shot, Inspector."

That was bad, McKernan thought. People on Mars weren't supposed to have guns. With the thin skins of most buildings and a hostile atmosphere outside that would support life exactly as long as you could hold your breath, they were dangerous, and not just to the targets. The Authority had made them illegal and the corporations had been more than willing to agree. They weren't easy to get—not something that could be picked up casually or made, like a knife. Even without the details it sounded like the work of a real criminal and not just a squabble over a claim or a woman.

"Okay. Let me have the report. I'll take a look at it."

He took the folder from Ferris who looked a bit crestfallen. *He probably expects me to go rush off to the outside and track down the murderer like an Indian scout,* McKernan thought. *He'd learn in time.* Mars was a big planet and a dangerous one, but because of its nature there were also very few places that a man could run to and none where he could hide indefinitely.

He was leafing through the report when he came to his door. For the thousandth time he read, "Inspector Erik McKernan, Chief Constable." *Mother would have been proud,* he thought sardonically. She had hated the L.A. cops like all the other residents of the barrio. He went through the door into the little cubicle that was his real home. There, sitting at his desk, he began to read the report, sketchy though it was, to look for some explanations.

The Blood Red Sands of Mars c is available now from The Fictional Press. Find it on TheFictionalPress.com, or buy it on Amazon.com!

THE FICTIONAL DETECTIVE
BY GREG FOWLKES

WHO KILLED EZEKIAL O. HANDLER?

A beautiful dame, a hard-boiled private eye --- and a dead body.

It started like any other case. When a famous writer dies in a mysterious car crash, private detective Frank Slade is called in to find answers, but all he finds is more questions. Who killed Ezekial Handler? Who is Janet Nielsen and why is she so interested in finding out? Who is leaving the neatly typed clues? And as Slade tries to find answers to these questions he starts to wonder if the ultimate answer will threaten his very existence.

Now available from The Fictional Press.
Buy it on Amazon.com!

The Laws of Magic
By Greg Fowlkes

Egil Njalson was an aspiring lawyer. A lawyer with a difference. Not only had he passed the bar, but he had an undergraduate degree from the most prestigious school of magic in the country, the California Institute of Thaumaturgy. Needless to say his caseload and clients tended to the unusual. Like witches; or vampires. And the opposition, well they were likely to be demons. But Egil Njalson had sworn an oath to uphold the law of the land, and...

The Laws of Magic

Now available from The Fictional Press.
Buy it on Amazon.com!

The Fictional Press
www.TheFictionalPress.com

About The Fictional Press

The Fictional Press, an imprint of Intrepid Ink, LLC, provides full publishing services to authors of fiction and non-fiction books, eBooks and websites. From editing to formatting, to publishing, to marketing, Intrepid Ink gets your creative works into the hands of the people who want to read them.

Find out more at www.thefictionalpress.com.

www.ingramcontent.com/pod-product-compliance
Lightning Source LLC
Chambersburg PA
CBHW070108030726
47506CB00002B/641